Barmy
Qua

About the Author

J. H. Brennan is one of those peculiar people who seem to be living in several different worlds at once.

He has always been interested in magic, spells and wizardry and has written a number of books on magic. He is also the author of several Fantasy Role-Playing Games, including the highly successful *Grailquest* series published by Armada.

Return of Barmy Jeffers and the
Quasimodo Walk

The Grailquest series

The Castle of Darkness
The Den of Dragons
The Gateway of Doom
Voyage of Terror
Kingdom of Horror
Realm of Chaos
Tomb of Nightmares
Legion of the Dead

Monster Horrorshow

Horror Classics

Dracula's Castle
The Curse of Frankenstein

J. H. Brennan

Barmy Jeffers and the Quasimodo Walk

ARMADA

First published in Armada in 1988 by
William Collins Sons & Co. Ltd.

Armada is an imprint of the Children's Division,
part of the Collins Publishing Group
8 Grafton Street, London W1X 3LA

Printed and bound in Great Britain by
William Collins Sons & Co. Ltd, Glasgow

One

Barmy Jeffers developed the Quasimodo Walk very early in life, encouraged by the fact that it enraged his sister.

She was a real threat, even in the days before she could crawl out of her cot. She'd lie there swaddled in pink, beadying at him with dark, piggy eyes and laying on him the curses she remembered from her last incarnation as a witch. Before she could talk she made him break a teapot, sprain a wrist, twist an ankle, forget his homework and fall off his bike innumerable times. There was no way of avoiding the curses, and no point in complaining to disbelieving parents. But the Quasimodo Walk evened things up a bit.

Barmy would lurk at the point furthermost from the cot, hanging about with enormous patience until her eyes lighted on him. They said little kids couldn't focus all that well, but Lauren locked on like a laser and stayed locked on until she lost interest, usually only when you left the room. Barmy waited for the lock on, then grimaced horribly, contorted his body and began the Quasimodo Walk.

As Barmy lurched towards her, left knee bent, hands curled into claws, right shoulder raised, right foot trailing, right eye wide, left eye shut, lips curled and drooling, breath hissing and rattling through clenched teeth, Lauren would begin to pound her bedclothes with small, impotent fists while her complexion changed gradually from cherubic rose to fiery red (and on a good day, blue), at which time she would emit a werewolf howl of fury.

Once she was sufficiently wound up to keep going for a bit, Barmy would rearrange his face and body and leave the room, whistling lightly, while his mother thundered downstairs to find out what was upsetting her little darling now.

Barmy's old man was a systems analyst for IBM, which meant the house was full of computers – not all of them IBMs – and empty of Barmy's old man. Most of the time he lived in aeroplanes, aimed at the mainframes of the world where he was paid vast sums to trouble-shoot applications in Fortran or Pascal. With so much hardware about, Barmy spoke Applesoft, Logo, Forth and 6502 Assembler like a native, but had no ambition to follow in his father's footsteps.

When she wasn't thundering downstairs, Barmy's mother was the sort of woman who draws wolf whistles from construction workers. The only woman Barmy had ever seen to match her was Queen Nefertiti, who was too long dead to provide much real competition.

On the odd occasions when she dressed up to go out, she would pirouette like a model and say, "How do I look, Barney?"

And Barmy would reply, "You look very nice, Mother."

He was less enamoured of Lauren. As she grew, Lauren progressed from mute witchcraft to physical assaults like spitting in his eye and throwing her meal down his shirt-front. Then, quite suddenly, she stopped all that and became intellectual and sly. At an age when most little girls were content to sit in muddy puddles, Lauren learned to read and, as her coordination improved, play the cello. One or other of these occupations ruined her eyesight so that she was forced to wear little wire-frame granny glasses. Apart from that, she was slim and blonde and frighteningly intelligent, her head stuffed with all sorts of things that even adults didn't know. She was also an aggro merchant. In certain of her moods, Barmy feared her as he feared vampires.

Barmy was well aware of the emotional perils of his situation and even recognized the roots of most of them. He missed his old man. He felt put down by his sister. He was jealous of his mother's affections (and loathed construction workers). Often he experienced that strange feeling all young men have when confined to a predominantly female household. He sometimes wished he had been born a woman himself, or possibly a spider. But most of the time he simply wanted to be a hero.

Being a hero, however, was an occupation for which he was frankly ill-equipped. Although durable enough in a wiry sort of way, he was not big, not sporty and totally unskilled in the ways of battle, as the encounter with Lugs Brannigan clearly indicated.

He met up with Lugs in the school yard and found himself immediately involved in one of those ominous, nerve-wracking conversations which begin:

"Here, who are you looking at?"

"Who, me, Lugs?"

"Yes, you, Creepo."

"Nobody, Lugs. I wasn't looking at – "

"Yes, you were. You were looking at me, weren't you, Creepo?"

"No, honest, Lugs, I wasn't – "

And so on until Lugs established sufficient reason to beat him to a pulp.

The incident was not only brutally unfair, but was destined to become fearfully embarrassing as well since Lauren became enraged that anyone should dare to strike her brother (a privilege jealously reserved for herself) and so terrorized Lugs Brannigan with her acid tongue that he actually sought out Barmy and apologized. It was mortifying.

To compensate for this sort of grot, Barmy took up Fantasy Role Play. He discovered a shop called *The Diceman* which specialized in games and novelties and slipped in to search for some nasty little gift for his headmaster. He came out instead with a boxed set of *Dungeons & Dragons*.

After that, Barmy started to live two lives, one in a world where you could spot the teachers by the leather patches on their elbows, the other where you buckled on your armour, took up your trusty +3 sword and went underground to hack up things like wyverns and gelatinous cubes.

Inevitably, his mother worried, as mothers always do when you're enjoying yourself. Having read numerous books on child psychology, she decided to have an adult conversation with him. During this, she pointed out the dangers of his fantasy world spilling over into reality, possibly even interfering with his studies.

Barmy reassured her that he knew the difference between an imaginary ghoul and Mr Parke's Doberman and she seemed satisfied. In fact, he was telling no more than the truth. He had no difficulty distinguishing between fantasy and reality; and that, to some extent, was his trouble. He had become a hero inside his head (where his rotten little sister couldn't turn up to rescue him) but somehow it wasn't enough. What he wanted was to be a hero in the real world, maybe even rescue Lauren for a change. He never thought it would happen, not any of it.

But that was before he knew about the Möbius Warp inside the old Logan place and certainly before he Quasimodo Walked right through it.

Two

The old Logan place looked a bit like the house in *Psycho*. It was on top of a hill, very isolated, and made a great creepy silhouette against the night sky. The Logans were long gone, of course, having emigrated to Darwin, Australia, and the house had been empty ever since. One summer, Fergo Franklin started the rumour it was haunted.

Fergo was a fat, sweaty boy who spent a lot of time by himself and rambled erratically. One of his rambles brought him to the old Logan place where – so he told everybody later – he saw a skeletal figure, near-nude and deathly white, flitting about the second storey.

As you might expect, Fergo ran, and having retraced his way to civilization became unusually sociable, gripping arms wherever he could find them and telling his story with saucer eyes. Not a lot of people believed him, because not a lot of people believed in ghosts. Part of the trouble was the way Fergo told the story. He used phrases like *glistening fangs* and *fiery eyes*, and nobody talks like that unless they're telling lies.

Maybe he would have convinced more people eventually, but he didn't have the time. Eight days after he saw the Thing at the Logan house, Fergo disappeared. Andy Lee reckoned the creature had got him, fiery eyes and glistening fangs and all, but since the rest of his family disappeared at the same time, the consensus was that the Franklins had simply left the district.

Fergo's story did better in his absence than when he was around to tell it. Everyone had a different version but the only person who dared to find out the truth was Barmy Jeffers, who didn't need urging to live up to his nickname. To be fair, he was driven almost as much by curiosity as an urge for glory. The *Monster Manual* of *D & D* had lots of illustrations of things that crawled from crypts, but this was the first time he had even a remote opportunity of seeing one in the flesh. The *rotting* flesh, he muttered darkly to Lauren, hoping to impress her; as usual without success. Chances are he did not really believe it himself, otherwise he wouldn't have gone: he wasn't that brave. But he believed Fergo had seen something, even if it was only an overgrown crow, and he knew his stock would rise if he went to investigate. In a sense, he was still seeking the road that would lead to his becoming a hero. And in a sense, of course, he'd found it.

Not being completely daft, he went out to the old Logan place in the early morning, which is the last time you'd expect to find any undead up and active. He left his bike at the bottom of the hill, propped against the pole that held the peeling FOR SALE sign, and walked the rest of the way, dodging from bush to shrub like an Indian scout. He felt pleasantly tense, deliciously apprehensive, tastily fearful. What he did not feel was terrified. Close up, the Logan place looked what it was: an eccentric old house going fast to seed because nobody lived in it.

The path led past what used to be a vegetable plot, now overgrown, and ended in an open courtyard where the gravel layer was losing a fight against the weeds.

Barmy spent quite a long time trying to figure out how to get inside the Logan house. The broken windows were not much help since they were the old-fashioned type, divided into nine small panes with no room to squeeze through unless you were prepared to smash the wood. There was a skylight which might be ajar, but the only access to it was a rusty drainpipe which was far too treacherous to climb. He circled the whole place twice, lost in thought. In the end, having given up all hope, he pushed the front door and found it open.

Whatever the time of day or outside appearance, the inside of a deserted house is always a bit creepy and Barmy found himself trying to move quietly and actually holding his breath when he opened a door.

The Logans had sold off most of the furniture when they emigrated, but a few tatty bits and pieces remained, sometimes enough to identify the usage of a room. This might have been a living room. That could have been a study, this was obviously the kitchen, judging by the plumbing. And so on.

Upstairs was not so easy, for every room he entered was stripped down to the bare boards. This was where the Thing was supposed to have walked, so he proceeded with exaggerated caution. But however tremulously he walked, nothing reached out to grab him. Eventually he found his way into the room overlooking the courtyard, the very room (he had deduced from the description) where Fergo had seen the pale figure. It was empty, at least of ghouls, but with more than enough of other things to explain the mystery.

There was a heap of straw over by one wall, and a small, rickety table and a wooden stool. There was a billycan and a chipped enamel mug. Most important of all, there was the debris people leave behind when they eat: brightly coloured wrappers, crushed cans, cardboard tubs, paper bags and the rest. Maybe it was picnickers, which Barmy thought unlikely, or a vagrant or two or a hippie-style commune, but it certainly wasn't Dracula, who had never been known to sink his teeth into a Big Mac, however underdone.

Immediately, Barmy felt tension drain away. In his

head, he was rehearsing the story he would tell to his friends, how he had arrived at midnight, determined to confront the Fiend, only to discover it was no more than an undercoloured old tramp. He thought of Fergo skulking in the bushes and giggled. A figure passing the window was all he'd needed: his nerves had done the rest.

He found himself exploring the remainder of the house as if he lived there. And just to encourage the imaginary Fergo, Barmy assumed his monstrous Quasimodo Walk and, one foot dragging, started down the stairs.

Three

Barmy fell, but only a few centimetres, so the sensation was more of a jolt than anything. Something else must have happened as well, for after the fall, short though it was, he landed outside, in the sturdy branches of an ancient oak tree which was definitely not growing in the grounds of the old Logan place, but seemed instead to be part of a dense forest. He shook his head, squeezed his eyes shut then opened them again, but it made no difference. He was wedged into a thick fork in the branches of an oak tree. One minute he was walking (well, Quasimodo Walking) downstairs in the Logan house, the next he was in a tree, outside somewhere. He was starting to wonder about loss of memory when the wolves diverted his attention.

They had probably been there all the time, but had been keeping quiet about it. Now, however, a couple of them decided it was time to terrify their prey and howled. It was a chilling sound. Barmy had read about wolf howls, heard a few in movies, even imitated them himself, but nothing matched the reality for sheer blood-curdling terror. His body froze into total immobility, but his head was silly enough to look down. The pack was milling at the bottom of the tree, sinister grey shapes which paced restlessly, glancing up occasionally, snapping and snarling amongst themselves in frustration. They had amber eyes.

With nothing better to do, Barmy closed his own eyes again and shivered. He opened them in time to see a wolf attempting to climb the tree – leaping at the bole and scrabbling with its forelegs – fortunately without success.

13

Like its colleagues, it looked at least twice as big as any of the wolves he had seen at the zoo.

"Shoo!" Barmy shouted, indicating he could be as stupid as the next lad when his brains were scrambled with fright. Predictably, the wolves ignored him.

From somewhere deep inside himself he found the courage to move. Not much, not out of the fork and certainly not off the branch, but enough to ease a numbness in his right foot (the one he had been dragging in the Quasimodo Walk) and set up pins and needles in his left hand.

He wondered how he had got here. Making sure he was still firmly wedged, he pushed himself upright, looped one arm over a branch for further security and looked around. There was no sign of the old Logan place. In fact, there was no sign of anything at all except forest trees. And wolves.

Where was he? He found himself screaming the question inside his head. Where was he? There was no forest near the old Logan place, not even a wood. And as far as Barmy knew, there was no such thing as an oak forest *anywhere*. And even if he was wrong about the forests and the oaks, he knew, he positively *knew* wolf packs were a thing of the past round here. What he didn't know was where round here actually was.

Ooowwoooooooooo!

He did not look down and was rather pleased to note the howl had not paralysed him with fright this time. He still had the use, more or less, of his body. Although what use it was going to be to him was another question. He began to fumble in his pockets to see if he was carrying a machine-gun.

He had a great deal of string, one length of it threaded through a battered conker. He had a small stone, veined with some glittering material he had once suspected might

14

be gold. He had his bright red Swiss Army penknife, which included tiny scissors and a corkscrew – just the thing for seeing off a pack of giant wolves. He had part of a cheese sandwich wrapped up in paper. In the circumstances, it was not a lot to go on.

"Shoo!" he said again. And to his absolute astonishment, the entire pack took off into the forest, yelping in total panic.

For a long time, Barmy did not move.

He listened. There was a fair bit of noise in the forest, but most of it was coming from the wolf pack's panicked flight, yipping and yelping, but definitely receding. Any suspicion he might have had about their lying in wait for him dispersed like fog. After a while, heart thumping, he climbed down the tree.

The forest floor was thick with leaf mould, forming a springy carpet which deadened his footsteps. There were no roads, not even clearly defined paths, just places where the undergrowth was easier to get through than others. And he became aware of something else as well: a sudden change in the weather. On his sortie to the Logan house, it had been overcast, but warm. Here, in the forest, he could not see the sky, but there was a distinct nip in the air; all right so long as he kept moving, but enough to chill him if he stayed still for too long.

Not that he planned to stay still. Even the lack of a path did not hassle him. There was only one direction he could possibly go – the opposite way to the wolf pack. He made no attempt to disguise the sound of his passage, or cover his tracks, or blaze his trail, or do any of the sensible things people always did in films when caught up in disasters. All he wanted was to generate distance.

He had only gone a few hundred metres when he broke into a clearing and discovered why the wolf pack had fled.

There was a weasel in the clearing. More accurately,

there was a weasel *filling* the clearing: it was as long as an elephant and stood half as high. The wolf pack had presumably scented the monster and taken off for parts unknown. Barmy could not altogether blame them: nothing, but nothing, was going to come out on top of that brute.

He stared in disbelief. Weasels, he knew, were vicious little beasts, but the emphasis was definitely on little. He had never heard of one much bigger than a cat, and you never heard of a weasel killing anybody because weasels just weren't big enough. Except this weasel was big enough. Big enough to kill you, big enough to eat a wolf pack.

The weasel turned to look at him and he did the only thing possible for an apprentice hero. He ran.

Exhaustion claimed him eventually and he collapsed, gasping, his arms embracing the trunk of a tree for support. But even over his rasping breath and thumping heart he realized there was no pursuit. If there was any benefit at all to be derived from being chased by a giant weasel, it was that you could at least hear the thing coming.

As he caught his breath, he tried to figure out what was going on. One minute in the Logan house, the next minute out here in some stupid forest. Nothing in between – but that was impossible. There *had* to be something in between such as him coming all the way down the Logan stairs and leaving the Logan property and walking, or cycling or hitching a lift here and climbing a tree to get away from the . . . he didn't want to think too much about that.

Amnesia had to be the best bet. A sudden blackout of the memory, like a power cut when you were watching TV. It had to be something like that. Something pulled the power plug on his memory, so there was a big black

16

gap between the Logan house and here. Except where did that leave a giant weasel? You'd have to have a pretty lousy memory to forget there were things that big in forests.

He began to move again, not because he knew where to go, but because he was nervous. After fifty metres, helped by the luck of the devil, he emerged from the forest.

Four

There was a road. Not a good road, but a road. Bits of it
were beaten earth, bits of it were cobbled and all of it was
in fiercely bad repair, but it was more than wide enough
to take a cart or a carriage and like most roads, it ran two
ways at once, presenting Barmy with the problem of
which direction to take.

As he hesitated, the broad sweep of the forest at his
back and what looked like wasteland everywhere else,
stretching to the purple of some not-too-distant mountains, he wondered what had put carts and carriages into
his head. Just looking at that road, he couldn't imagine a
car on it, not even a Land Rover or a Jeep. All he could
imagine was a cart or carriage.

There was no sign of the old Logan place, no sign of any
stretch of countryside that was even remotely familiar.
Judging by the sun, which was past its zenith, the road
ran more or less north/south. He wished he had a coin to
help him decide on a direction. He remained locked by
indecision for perhaps another thirty seconds, then,
driven by the fear of weasel or wolves emerging from the
forest, he struck north.

An hour later, Barmy was tired, hungry, frightened and
bad-tempered. He had distanced himself from the forest,
but the road got no better and seemed to be running
through deserted scrubland. Not a house, not a bungalow,
not a cottage to be seen: not even a ploughed field or a
tractor. No people, no horses, no livestock. Neither a car
– nor cart – came down the road. He was utterly, totally

alone. And, though he preferred not to think about it, utterly and totally lost.

After another hour, the sun was definitely setting. He was a lot more nervous now and worried what would happen if he was stuck out here after dark. By the time another hour had passed, he seemed in grave danger of finding out. He had reached the mountain chain and the road had plunged into a steep valley, gloomy and oppressive, with the light fading by the second. A wind had sprung up, moaning down the valley from the north and occasionally making funny ghost noises.

Barmy pulled himself together and plodded on. Soon, it grew so dark he had to slow his pace almost to a crawl for fear of losing the road. He knew he would have to stop shortly, camp out for the night, but the thought appalled him. In a country of wolves and giant weasels, it was not difficult to imagine what might come out after dark; only difficult to imagine what to do about it. Worse still, there seemed to be absolutely nowhere suitable to stop, no sheltered cranny, no cave, not even a tree he could climb for safety from the wolves.

He was just about ready to give up when he suddenly saw a light. At first he thought it might be wishful thinking. Then he convinced himself it was a firefly or a glow-worm.

Eventually, what had at first appeared to be a single light resolved itself into many. He came closer still then stopped, seized by a sensation of alarm. He now knew for certain that he had landed somewhere very different from the old Logan place. At the end of the road, completely blocking the valley ahead, was a looming medieval keep, its grim, castellated walls weirdly illuminated by banks of flaming torches set into iron brackets.

Barmy gaped. The last time he had seen anything like this was in a film about King Arthur; and even then the

cinematographic version was not a patch on the reality.
Or as creepy. The walls were more sturdy than those of
any building he had ever known; cyclopean masonry
constructed of gigantic granite blocks, grimy, soot-stained
and looking as if they hadn't moved since Adam trekked
off out of Eden.

His eyes swept upwards to what seemed like battlements, but even in the flickering torchlight the walls were
so high it was impossible to be certain what was up there.
He allowed his gaze to drift back down. At the end of the
road he had followed for so long was a broad cobbled
courtyard which approached two massive, iron-studded
wooden gates set into the castle wall.

Barmy's fearful, trance-like state broke abruptly and he
began to run, something he would not have believed
possible five minutes before. However weird, however
unexpected, here was shelter, here was food and, above
all, here was information. Of the many things Barmy
wanted to know at that moment, the most important was
where he was and how he got here and especially how
soon he could get back.

His shoes rattled on the cobbles and then he was
pour ding his fists on the wooden gate. He noticed a small
door to the right, set into the main structure, and beside
it a sliding panel, presumably used as a peephole.

"Hello!" called Barmy. "Hello! Hello! Hello!"

Thump! Thump! Thump!

"Anybody home?" called Barmy.

Thump! Thump! Thump! Thump! Thump!

"Let me in!" called Barmy. Out of nowhere, the
thought occurred to him it might be a monastery. Lots of
really old castles were taken over by monks nowadays
and used as monasteries, so that even though they looked
sinister, they weren't really: just warm, comfortable
places where kindly monks would give you a bowl of soup

20

and ring your parents to get the car out and come fetch you any time of . . .

The peephole opened abruptly.

"Oh boy!" gasped Barmy. "Am I glad to see you! My name's Barney Jeffers . . . I was over at the old Logan place you know the one Fergo Franklin said was haunted . . . I was coming out and somehow I got lost I think it might have been amnesia . . . I got chased up a tree by wolves only they were chased away by a giant weasel . . . I ran out of the forest and found the road . . . I've been walking for hours only I never thought I'd ever see anybody again . . . this really is a desolate bit of the country isn't it?" He drew breath. "Anyway, can I come in? I've got nowhere to stay for the night and my folks must be worried sick by now so maybe you could phone them and – "

"Get lost!" growled a rough voice from within.

Barmy stopped his monologue abruptly. "What?" he asked. It hadn't sounded like a monk.

"Go orn, go away!" the rough voice rasped. "I know your tricks."

"Tricks?" echoed Barmy. "I'm not playing – "

"You're a ghoul ain't yer? Something your shape would have to be a ghoul. What's wrong – not enough corpses out there for your dinner?"

"Ghoul?" Barmy blinked in astonishment. "I'm not a ghoul!"

"Wraith. Is it a wraith? You look a bit solid for a wraith."

"I'm a boy!" shouted Barmy.

"More like a werewolf," the rough voice said speculatively. "Only I didn't think the moon was full tonight."

"I'm not a werewolf!" Barmy howled. "I'm not a ghoul, I'm not a wraith, I'm not a werewolf!"

"Vampire, then. It's got to be a vampire this time of

night. Nothing in here for you, vampire, so you just creep back to your crypt and – "

"I'm not a vampire!" Barmy shrieked. "Are you blind or just looneytunes? Can't you *see*?"

For the first time a touch of uncertainty invaded the rough voice. "You just come over here under the light." Barmy moved promptly to take his place before the peephole. "Orl right," said the voice cautiously. "Snarl!"

"Snarl?" asked Barmy.

"Yus."

Barmy snarled.

There was a lengthy silence. Eventually the voice said, "You don't have vampire teeth, I'll give you that. Ghoul teeth neither. Let me see the palms of your hands."

Obediently, Barmy held up his hands, palms outwards.

"No hair," muttered the voice. "So you ain't a were-wolf. And your third finger's shorter than the middle finger, which rules out dopplegangers and barrow-wights. You haven't got wings, so you can't be a balrog. What did you say you was?"

"A boy!" Barmy gasped. "I'm a boy!"

"You just wait there," the rough voice rasped. And the peephole closed abruptly, leaving Barmy alone in the sudden silence and the flickering torchlight.

Five

Barmy waited for what seemed like years, then the peephole opened again, so abruptly that it made him jump.

"What?" asked a voice, a shade less rough, but a shade more irritable than the last. "What? What?"

"What?" asked Barmy.

"This idiot tells me you're not a vampire," said the voice.

"I'm not," Barmy confirmed. "I'm not anything."

"Snarl," instructed the voice irritably.

"Look, sir," said Barmy patiently, "I've already done all that – "

"Yus," said the original voice, "we've been through all that, Your Holiness. Little pearly teef, no fangs, no hair on 'is palms, fingers all the right length, that's why I thought I'd better wake you, sir."

"Sir," said Barmy, "all I need is shelter and to know where I am and maybe – "

"Thing is," said the original voice, "supposing he really is human, can't leave him out there, can we? Not at night. Wouldn't last beyond an hour at – "

"I am human! Can't you see I'm – "

"Teeth aren't everything," said the new voice. "And he might have shaved the palms of his – "

"I didn't!" Barmy screamed. "I don't shave. I'm not old enough to shave."

"Yus, but if he hasn't got the teeth he's not a vampire or a ghoul and it's not full moon – "

"As Keep Secretary, it is my duty – "

23

"I just want to come in. There are wolves out – "

" – looks sort of foreign to me, as if he doesn't rightly belong, but I don't think he's – "

" – question of finance and accommodation and – "

" – been walking for hours – "

In the middle of it all, the small door in the main gate suddenly opened with a scrabbling of bolts. A broad hand reached out and dragged Barmy through. The door slammed behind him at once and the bolts were shot back, one following another like rifle shots.

He was in an enclosed, stone-flagged courtyard, well lit by wall torches. His nose told him there might be stable accommodation somewhere to his right, and an archway directly ahead led into a gloomy tunnel. From in here he could see there were battlements above; and guarded too, judging by the shadowy figures which were parading to and fro. Beside him, broad hand still clamped fiercely on his shoulder, was a soldier, thickly muscular and beetle-browed with close-cropped salt and pepper hair, but a soldier who must have missed the latest updates in equipment since he was carrying – of all things – a crossbow and a sword. Worse, he was wearing armour. Not full armour, admittedly, not Knight of the Round Table stuff, but a breastplate and helmet, with a sort of heavy leather kilt over sackcloth leggings bound criss-cross with thongs.

"Orl right," he said. "You're in now, so shut your face."

Barmy's eyes swung to the second figure. This one looked an even bigger lunatic than the first: a tall, thin, slightly stooping individual with a straggly wisp of grey-white beard. Unlike the guard, he wore no armour, but was instead dressed in a tasselled nightcap, a white and blue striped flannel nightshirt and a pair of heavy leather boots. He carried an oil lamp, the flame of which had blown out.

"Human?" asked this apparition.

Barmy nodded. "Yes." It had occurred to him that monks weren't the only ones who took over old castles. Psychiatrists sometimes did as well. A small chill of fear crawled up the base of his spine. Maybe he would have been safer with the wolves. Then he remembered the weasel and decided he was doing nicely where he was.

A skinny finger reached out to poke Barmy in the chest. "Solid," said the man in the nightshirt. He turned to the guard. "Not a wraith – solid."

"Yus," the guard said.

"So, what? You're human, eh?" the man in the nightshirt said to Barmy. "Well, answer me one thing: what were you doing in the Wilderness?"

"Excuse me, sir," said Barmy cautiously, "but who are you?" He held his breath, mentally giving odds the answer would be something like Napoleon.

"Bong," said the man in the nightshirt.

"Bong?" asked Barmy. Maybe he believed he was a striking clock.

"This here's the Reverend Lancelot Bong," the guard explained. "Keep Secretary and Treasurer. Very important man around here."

"How do you do, Sir Lancelot," Barmy said politely.

"Not Sir, just Reverend," said the Bong. "They haven't knighted me just yet. Now what were you doing in the Wilderness? Quickly now – I want to go to bed."

So, Barmy realized, did he . . . badly. He wanted to climb under the sheets, pull the clothes over his head and sleep sound in the knowledge he was going to wake up at home with nothing worse to worry him than Lauren. He took a deep breath and told his story as best he could, painfully aware it sounded as odd as the Reverend Bong's nightcap. But he left nothing out, not even the silly bits.

25

In a situation like this, you never knew what might prove important.

"What's a Quasimodo Walk?" frowned Bong, when Barmy finally ground to a halt.

"It's a sort of mumblety – mumble thing I mumble, mumble," Barmy told him.

"What? Speak up! Couldn't hear a word you said."

"It's a sort of funny walk I invented to annoy my sister," Barmy muttered, reddening.

"Show me."

"Show you?"

"Yes," snapped the Reverend Bong. "Is it like this – ?" He began to march up and down the courtyard, nightshirt flying, in a passable imitation of an energetic German goose step. "Or like this – ?" He clasped his hands behind his back, stood on one leg and hopped. "Or like – "

"No, no," Barmy said hurriedly, suddenly fearful this old idiot was going to do himself a dreadful injury. He raised his shoulder, dragged his leg, clawed his hands, grimaced his face and shambled forward in the Quasimodo Walk.

"My gord!" exclaimed the guard.

But the Reverend Bong only watched him thoughtfully. "And you were like that when you were walking down the stairs in the Logan house?"

"Yes, sir," Barmy nodded.

"Sounds like a Möbius Warp to me," the Bong said, frowning.

"A what?" asked Barmy, suddenly excited. If anybody knew what had happened to him, that was progress.

But the Reverend Bong only said, "We'll talk about it in the morning."

Six

It wasn't that things looked better in the morning, but they certainly looked interesting. The castle was not a castle, at least not the sort of castle you read about. It was more like a small town, walled and garrisoned, with its own stores and living quarters. It didn't have a name as such: everybody Barmy talked to just called it the Keep or sometimes the Borderlands Keep.

The big news was that the Keep was situated in Magnum Varna, a Province of Macanna, largest of the Federated Isles of Skor; none of which Barmy had ever heard of. The Keep itself had been built at the head of the valley which was the only pass connecting the southern Wilderness with the fertile northlands. Its purpose was to keep the monsters out. Or in, depending on which side you happened to be talking about. But whichever side you were talking about, the monsters definitely inhabited the Wilderness which, Barmy realized with a shudder, was where he had found himself after leaving the Logan place.

The Reverend Lancelot Bong appeared for breakfast mercifully devoid of his nightshirt, which had been replaced by a jerkin, doublet and blouse over corduroy leggings and stylishly pointed elf shoes in green leather, presumably dyed. Slung from his belt were two daggers, a cudgel and a short sword.

"Church Militant," he said shortly, when he noticed Barmy eyeing the weaponry.

"I beg your pardon?"

"Church Militant," the Bong repeated. "I'm a member

27

of the Church Militant. Bless 'em, bash 'em, hack 'em, slash 'em – part of the new wave philosophy for dealing with the forces of evil."

"Does it work?" asked Barmy curiously.

"No, but it's fun."

Breakfast consisted of scrambled eggs, wild mushrooms and some sort of corned beef hash served up on dark, crumbly bread, all washed down with an acrid, bittersweet drink that looked like coffee, smelled like almonds and tasted like nothing Barmy had ever had before. Despite the bewilderment of his situation, he enjoyed every mouthful.

"Do you run the Keep, sir?" Barmy asked politely. He had abandoned the theory that the Reverend Bong was mad; or at least any madder than the rest of this weird place.

"Administration," said the Bong through a mouthful of mushroom. "The seneschal runs the military. The mayor is head of the civilian population. I look after the administration. And the church, of course – bless 'em, bash 'em, hack 'em, slash 'em."

"That must be a very important position," Barmy said, half because he meant it and half because it never did you any harm to butter people up.

"Yes," said the Reverend Bong. "Yes, it is. Very important. And boring. The Keep works far too well."

"Too well?"

"Not a monster's got through for fifteen years, except for the odd doppleganger. Not one's tried for five years until you turned up last night – and you're not really a monster, are you?"

"No," said Barmy uncertainly.

"There you are then," Bong said. "Boring."

Over the second cup of aquaria (the bittersweet drink) the conversation turned abruptly to Möbius Warps.

"Trans-dimensional distortions in the space-time continua, permitting relativistic anomalies involving quantum masses."

"Pardon?"

"Holes in space," the Bong said. "It's easily enough demonstrated." He pulled a sheet of parchment from his doublet, examined it briefly for matters of importance, then laid it on the table to cut a strip about five centimetres wide from one edge. Barmy winced as the sharp blade of the dagger ripped the tablecloth beneath, but the Bong did not seem to notice. "This," he said, "is a strip of parchment five centimetres wide and – what? – forty-five centimetres long. The size doesn't matter." He waved it about like a conjurer's rabbit.

He laid the strip down on the parchment and used it as a guide to cut another the same size, then another and another and another. "Whoops!" he said, as part of the tablecloth slid off onto the floor.

"So," said the Bong, having put away his dagger, "what have we here?"

"Several strips of paper the same size," said Barmy, wondering why so many people treated kids like idiots.

"Exactly!" said the Bong enthusiastically. "Now, we will take this strip and join one end to the other so that it forms a continuous band, a circle – " He used a little plum-red jam to make the join. Surprisingly, it worked extremely well, locking the two ends of paper like a colourful superglue. Barmy made a mental note to try something else on his toast.

"Now," said the Bong, putting the band to one side, "we will take a second strip and join it together like the first, but this time, before we do anything, we will put a twist in it." He did so, dabbed on the jam and made the join.

He looked at Barmy and grinned broadly as he picked up the first band. "A question for you: how many surfaces does this strip have?"

Barmy blinked. "Two," he said cautiously, suspecting a trick question although the answer seemed perfectly obvious. There was the surface on the outside of the circle and the surface on the inside, each corresponding to one side of the original strip of paper.

"Right!" exclaimed the Reverend Lancelot Bong. He picked up the second band and waved it under Barmy's nose. "And how many surfaces does this one have?"

"Two," Barmy said again, less cautiously this time.

"Wrong!" shouted the Bong, pounding the table excitedly. "It has one! It has one!"

"No, it hasn't," Barmy said. Any fool could see it had two, exactly like the other. "Any fo – anyone can see it has two."

"Ah, but it hasn't: that's the point. It's a Möbius strip and Möbius strips have only got one surface. Here, I'll prove it to you – " A stubby stick of charcoal emerged from the doublet and he passed both it and the Möbius strip to Barmy. "Take the first band – no, the first one – and put the charcoal down and draw a line on the outside. Keep going until it joins up."

Barmy did, suspiciously. When he had finished, a charcoal line divided the outside surface of the band like a railway track.

"What have you got?" asked the Bong.

"A band with a line on the outside," Barmy told him.

"Anything on the inside?"

"No, of course not."

The Bong sat back. "Do the same thing on the Möbius strip."

Barmy did, eyeing him suspiciously. Even before he had finished drawing, he knew he was into something

30

really weird. Just to make sure, he broke open both bands and spread them flat. The first had a line drawn on one side. The one that had formed the Möbius strip had a line that ran on *both* sides. It was impossible, but it had happened. He'd drawn both lines himself.

"You see?" said Bong. "You see?"

Barmy shook his head.

"There are two surfaces to reality!" exclaimed the Bong. "It's the only thing that makes sense! Most of the time you live on one surface and there's no way you can get to the other – it's as if you were living on the outside of that first band we made. But every so often, in certain places and under certain conditions, you get a sort of twist in space that converts reality into a Möbius strip. When that happens it's possible to get to the other side of reality the same way your charcoal line got to the other side of the paper. We call it a Möbius Warp. There must have been one in the old Logan place."

Barmy, who had followed the explanation quite well said, "So if I went back to the place where I came in to this reality and the Möbius Warp's still there, I should be able to get back to the Logan house?" He didn't relish the prospect of the wolf and weasel forest, but if it got him back to his own reality, he was willing to risk it. Maybe he could persuade the Reverend Bong to send some soldiers with him as protection.

But the Bong, who was reaching out to finish the last of the wild mushrooms, said, "I'm afraid it's not as simple as that."

Seven

Barmy's mind was full of Möbius Warps when the Reverend Bong turned him loose. It was not, as Bong had said, as simple as it sounded. First off, humans couldn't use them: only monsters could squeeze through a Möbius Warp. The fact that Barmy, who was almost certainly human, had got through one was probably attributable to the Quasimodo Walk, which gave him the temporary appearance of a monster.

Admittedly if the Walk had worked once, it could work again, but warps were one way only. The one in the Logan house led to the present reality, linking into a tree in the Wilderness forest. But even if you found the right tree and Quasimodo Walked along a branch, you still wouldn't get back to the Logan place. What you needed for that was to find a second Möbius Warp going in the opposite direction. If you Quasimodo Walked through that, then you got back to your own reality. Not necessarily to the Logan place, of course. The real problem was where to find a second Möbius Warp.

Although he seemed to know a lot about the warps, the Reverend Bong maintained he was no expert. If you wanted an expert in Möbius Warps, you talked to the alchemist Kendar. That was what Barmy was off to do now – trying to find Pitch Street, where the Alchemists' Guild was located; a likely place to learn the current whereabouts of Kendar. In order to ensure Barmy found Pitch Street quickly and easily, the Reverend Bong had written down detailed directions. Barmy followed them to the letter and was now completely lost.

Not that he was greatly hassled. He was enjoying his exploration of the Keep and when he really needed to find Pitch Street, he could always ask. In the meantime, he gawped at the passing parade of people and wondered vaguely where he might buy a pie.

He reached a sort of market square where there was a definite Fair Day atmosphere. This area was thronged with people and the noise was almost unbelievable. Merchant stalls, bright with flags and bunting, competed side by side while the merchants shouted themselves hoarse trying to attract more business. Pedlars who could not afford stalls sold off rolled-out carpets. Farmers sold vegetable products and some livestock direct from carts. And through all the hustle and bustle bounced brightly-dressed jugglers, sword-swallowers, fire-eaters and other entertainers, ready to seize any space available to put on a show for coins thrown by the crowd.

One such show was already underway when Barmy arrived, mounted by a tall, slim, upright man of immense dignity wearing multicoloured robes and a pointed hat. As Barmy edged his way through the crowd, he was causing a small birdcage to levitate some five feet off the ground – a really neat trick in Barmy's book.

"And now," said the tall man as the birdcage sank back down to the ground, "the Amazing Presto will attempt to perform the most astounding feat of legerdemain ever seen within the Federated Isles. I refer, ladies and gentlemen, to the incredible, the mind-bending, the remarkable . . . Andelusian Nigreto Basket Rope Illusion!" He whirled around dramatically and produced a wicker basket. Barmy was fascinated.

Surprisingly, the crowd actually thinned out, as if the Andelusian Nigreto Basket Rope Illusion was old hat to most of them. The Amazing Presto opened the lid of the basket and made mystic passes over it with slim violinist's hands. In a moment, a rope began to rise up out of the basket like some demented snake. At this point, Barmy felt somebody cut his purse.

Although he had arrived in Macanna with nothing more valuable than his champion conker, Barmy set out to explore the Keep with a silver coin and seven copper ones donated by the Reverend Bong, who had also given him a small leather purse to keep them in. As Barmy looked up he saw a smallish, red-haired figure now receding through the crowd, and he shouted, "Hey! Stop, thief!"

At this point, several things happened at once.

First off, the Amazing Presto cried, "Leave this to me!" At once the crowd around the red-haired man fell back, tripping and jostling in sudden panic. A dozen or more terrified voices shouted, "Presto – no!" The thief turned, eyes wide with horror and threw up his hands, as if to ward off an attack. Barmy launched himself forward to regain his purse.

"Metatron habet spengler domo!" intoned the Amazing Presto, raising both hands high above his head.

"Don't do it, Presto!" screamed a woman's voice.

A squat figure wearing leather armour stepped in front of Barmy, who cannoned into him, an experience similar in some respects to running full tilt into a brick wall.

"Squadrak shepla hara-hara grango!" Presto howled, his voice rising several registers. Above his head, a ghastly shape was forming in the air.

"He's calling up a slith!" somebody shouted in total panic. Immediately the entire square began to empty like magic. "Slith!" people screamed, "Slith! Slith!" Barmy tried to move, but the armour-clad figure flung two muscular arms around him, and with practised efficiency, wrestled him to the ground. The ghastly shape, a writhing mass of tentacles and fangs, launched itself forward, passing like an express train only inches above their heads. The thief screamed, dropped the purse and ran.

Pandemonium broke out in the square. The slith began to revolve rapidly on its own axis, apparently looking for the thief who had disappeared completely into the throng. Men and women were screaming, traders abandoned their stalls. The slith stopped revolving and, deprived of its thieving prey, suddenly struck out at the nearest structure, smashing it to matchwood. Tentacles scooped up pots, pans and ceramic jars and began to hurl them forcefully in all directions.

"Irate slith! Irate slith!" Dodging the missiles, the crowd was trampling itself half to death in a desperate attempt to get out of the square. Moving with incredible speed, the slith began to smash up several other stalls. From somewhere behind him, Barmy could hear the voice of the Amazing Presto intoning, "Vest tekram rettel crost. Vest tekram rettel crost."

As a space cleared around the slith, two armoured men ran forward, dropped to one knee and fired two crossbow bolts into the writhing body of the monster, without appreciable effect. Another stall splintered into match-wood. Howling like a terrified beast, the last of the crowd drained from the square and fled through the remainder of the town.

"Vest tekram rettel crost!"

Pinned though he was, Barmy had a clear view of the slith which, to his astonishment, began to lose substance, slowly at first, then more rapidly until it shimmered and faded out of existence with a faint pop and the acrid aroma of burning sulphur. A fat man bustled into the empty square, escorted by a small contingent of men at arms. "You'll pay for this!" he shrieked furiously at the Amazing Presto. "You'll pay for every scrap of damage, you bungling, incompetent – "

Barmy suddenly found he was free to get up and did so. To his surprise, he found the man who had flung him down out of the path of the slith stood half a head shorter than he did; a broad, heavily muscled, leather armoured, black bearded dwarven warrior with large brown eyes.

" – jailed for the next sixty years!" the fat man was screaming. "If I don't have you hanged, Presto! If I don't have you – "

The square looked like a bomb had hit it. Barmy's head turned slowly to take in the debris and the desolation.

" – throw away the key!" the fat man howled.

"Sliths are tricky to control," the dwarf remarked to Barmy.

Eight

It was the first time Barmy had ever been inside a tavern. He was considered too young to drink – at least back home. Here he might have toddled through the door wearing nappies for all anybody cared. It did not look like a law-abiding place. Several of the customers wore eye-patches, all were heavily armed and a few were falling-down drunk. Ben, the dwarf who had saved Barmy from collision with the slith, sat on the far side of the scrubbed pine table sinking pints of sour cider without any notice-able effect.

"What will happen to the Amazing Presto?" Barmy asked curiously. It was obvious to him now that the magician had somehow created the monster which wrecked the market square. Or if he hadn't, everybody believed he had, which amounted to much the same thing.

"They'll put him in jail until he finds enough money to pay for the damage," Ben said slowly. He seemed to do everything slowly, except in emergencies.

"When will that be?" Barmy asked.

"Never," Ben said, after careful consideration.

The information left Barmy feeling vaguely guilty – Presto had, after all, been trying to help him – but there was not a lot he could do about it. He fingered his purse, now recovered and retied to his belt, wondering if home would ever feel the same after all this excitement. The thought stimulated him to say, "Do you know where to find Pitch Street, Ben?"

"Yes," Ben said.

Barmy waited. After a while he said, "Can you tell me

how to get there – only I'm looking for an alchemist called Kendar and the Reverend Bong says the Alchemists' Guild will know where to find him."

"Is this to get you home?" asked Ben, who had heard Barmy's story while drinking his first pint of sour cider.

"Yes."

A concerned expression settled on Ben's features. "Kendar left the Keep seven weeks ago. I'm sorry, Barmy."

"Left?" Barmy echoed. He felt a sinking sensation in the pit of his stomach. "Where's he gone?"

There was a crash at a nearby table as two very large men started to fight. "Nobody knows," said Ben. He thought about it for a minute, then added, "not exactly."

"What exactly do you mean – not exactly?" Barmy asked. He had taken a liking to Ben, but found him difficult to follow at times.

Ben scratched the side of his nose thoughtfully. "He's become a hermit. Most alchemists do eventually – it gets them away from the fumes. They say he's living in a cave in the Pileggi Mountains. There are a lot of caves there."

"Where are the Pileggi Mountains?" Barmy asked.

"In the Wilderness," Ben said. He drained his tankard and refilled it from the jug. Without warning he smiled at Barmy. "I like sour cider – are you sure you don't want any?"

"No, thank you," Barmy said. He leaned across the table. "What am I going to do, Ben?"

"About what, Barmy?"

"The only way I can get home is through a Möbius Warp and the only one who knows anything about Möbius Warps is this bloke Kendar," Barmy said. "If I don't get hold of him, I'm stuck in this reality forever."

"Maybe you could come on the Facecrusher expedition," Ben suggested. "We're going quite close to the Pileggi Mountains."

"Expedition?" Barmy was at once interested and wary. As an afterthought he frowned. "Facecrusher?"

"Don't you have expeditions where you come from, Barmy?" Ben asked.

"I don't know. I don't think so. It depends what you mean."

"You'd like our expeditions," Ben said, his brown eyes lighting up a little. "We go into the Wilderness and bash monsters."

Barmy stared at him. After a moment he asked, "What's the point of that?"

Ben's grin widened. "Well, it's exciting, but that's not the point. No, the point is earning a living."

"You earn a living by bashing monsters?" He was beginning to realize that this place was a lot stranger than he'd originally imagined.

Ben shook his head. "We earn a living by finding gold. The monsters are fun, but incidental." He sat quite still for a very long time then just as Barmy was about to ask another question continued: "The Wilderness wasn't always a wilderness, Barmy. One time it had towns and villages and cities just like the rest of the country. But that was before the disaster."

"What disaster?" Barmy asked.

"I don't know," Ben said. "It was before my time. But the disaster turned the whole area into a wilderness and turned most things in it into monsters – vampires, werewolves and stuff like that."

"Giant weasels?"

"Yes, giant weasels. And ghouls. And Things. You never know what you'll find in the Wilderness. But the point is there's still a lot of gold there. Treasure. Jewels. Vron teeth. Bric –"

39

"Vron teeth?"

"Very valuable," Ben said. "When you can't find a steady job, there's always some expedition or other heading into the Wilderness in search of booty and you can join that. Facecrusher's is the next to go out."

"And I could join it?" Barmy asked, wondering if he was insane even to consider it.

"I'll have a word," promised Ben, "if you're interested." He hesitated thoughtfully. "Of course, you'll need to get the Reverend Bong's permission. He has the final say about who goes anywhere."

"Who's going on this expedition?"

"Well, Facecrusher's the leader, of course," Ben said. "You always have the biggest, roughest, toughest, meanest fighter as the leader and Facecrusher's all that, as well as having raised the money to equip us. Then there's me and another fighter called Pendragon. Then there's a thief called Rowan and – "

"Did you say thief?"

"To get us into the treasure vaults and avoid traps," Ben explained. "Thieves are good at that."

"But won't he steal your loot after you find it?" Barmy asked.

"Yes," Ben said.

After a bit, Barmy said, "Who else is on the expedition?"

"So far, the only other one is a woman called Aspen."

"What's she do?"

"Bashes monsters," Ben said. "Some women are very good at bashing monsters."

Thinking of Lauren, Barmy nodded.

"We really need a priest," Ben said, "but we haven't found one yet." For once he caught Barmy's expression and added, "You need a priest for healing. And if he's no good at healing, he can always bury you." He scratched his nose again. "And Facecrusher says we'd be better off with a wizard, but we haven't found one yet and – "

"Couldn't you take the Amazing Presto?" Barmy asked.

Ben began to giggle. "Very good, Barmy," he said, although Barmy did not realize he had made a joke. When he sobered up, Ben said, "We're off in three days' time. Do you think you'd like to join us, Barmy?"

"But isn't it terribly dangerous in the Wilderness?" Barmy frowned.

Two bodies locked in combat dropped from nowhere onto the table between them, smashing it like matchwood. Daggers flashed as the combatants attempted to stab each other.

Ben stood up. "Isn't it everywhere?" he said.

Nine

"But are you sure they'll let me go along?" Barmy asked a little desperately. What he really wanted to know was where the money was going to come from for all the equipment he was buying.

"You leave all that to me, Barmy," Ben told him with the sort of reassuring smile that makes you want to run away. They were in the store of Harkaan the Armourer, an emporium which smelled of metal, leather and sweat, the latter originating from Harkaan himself, a man who looked like a blacksmith gone to seed.

So far, at Ben's urging, Barmy had committed himself to a short sword, a mace, a dagger and a metal helmet which came down the front to cover his nose. Harkaan, who talked with a gravelly voice, was currently showing him a suit of chain mail at a cost of thirty silver pieces.

"Specially made, this was," Harkaan was saying, "for Acto the Unlucky. You remember Acto, don't you, Ben – he walked backwards into an alligator."

Ben nodded. "Yes."

Barmy coughed. "Could I have a word with you, Ben?"

"Yes, Barmy," Ben said, fingering a crossbow.

"In private," Barmy said firmly.

Ben looked up at him in surprise. "All right, Barmy."

They withdrew together out of earshot of Harkaan, who pretended to examine some gauntlets.

"Ben," Barmy said, "I can't afford all this stuff. To be honest, I can't afford any of this stuff. I've only got some coppers and a silver piece the Reverend Bong gave me. I might just manage a down payment on the dagger, but everything else – '

"Oh, you mustn't worry about that, Barmy," Ben said in sudden concern. "Anything you get is charged to Facecrusher at the beginning of the expedition and then deducted from your share of the booty when we find it. I thought you knew."

"No," Barmy said, relieved. Then he glanced at the arms and armour and got uptight again. "But suppose Facecrusher doesn't want me on the expedition?"

"If you're not on the expedition, which you will be, Barmy, never fear; you don't collect the stuff you're buying now and Facecrusher doesn't pay for it. We only collect our stuff the day before we're due to set out. Don't worry, Barmy." He gripped Barmy's elbow and led him back to Harkaan. "My friend will take the chain mail, Harkaan," he said.

The grand total, by the time he had finished, amounted to one hundred and twenty-seven silver pieces. This worried Barmy a lot more than it worried Ben, who insisted he would be able to pay it back out of the first treasure chest with enough left over to equip himself a second time around. None of it stopped Barmy fretting.

"You're a real old misery, Barmy," Ben said testily as they left the store. "If you don't believe me, why don't we just go see Facecrusher now."

"It's not that I don't believe you, Ben," Barmy reassured him, lying through his teeth. "It's just that I've never been on an expedition before and I'm new around here and I'm not even in my own world and that makes me nervous. But I do believe you, honest I do – "

"Only you'd rather hear it from Facecrusher."

"Yes," Barmy said.

"You just follow me," said Ben.

Following Ben took him into a warren of narrow

43

alleyways, across a cobbled courtyard and down a broad flight of worn stone steps. They stopped before a tiny shop with an apothecary sign outside. Through the grimy little diamond panes of the window, Barmy could see a display of bowls and boxes containing variously coloured powders. He noticed one was labelled Ground Mummy. Ben pushed the door, which sounded a jangling bell as he entered.

Behind the counter, a grey-haired woman was perched on a low stool knitting something shapeless. "Hello, Ben," she said.

"Hello, Facecrusher," Ben replied.

Facecrusher? This was Facecrusher? Barmy blinked in the gloom.

"This is my friend Barmy," Ben was saying. "He is young, but he is a lethal fighting machine capable of disembowelling a dragon with his bare hands. Only days ago he put an entire wolf pack to flight and saw off a giant weasel. Furthermore, he is skilled in sorcery, magic, voodoo, witchcraft and conjuration. He wants to join our expedition. What do you say, Facecrusher?"

The woman set down her knitting and stood up. Barmy followed the movement and found himself looking up and up and up at one of the largest, widest human beings he had ever seen. He noticed she was wearing a metal breastplate under her woollen cardigan. A hand the size of a ham came across the counter to swallow his own in a vigorous shake. "Good to have you with us, Barmy," Facecrusher grinned.

Barmy's mouth was still hanging open as he staggered out into the sunlight. He walked nearly a hundred metres before he collected himself enough to say, "What did you tell her that for?"

"Tell her what, Barmy?" Ben asked.

"That I could tear dragons apart and work magic. I

44

don't know anything about magic." He felt himself becoming hysterical, but could do nothing to stop it. "Why did you tell her all that stuff, Ben? Why? Why did you say that?"

"So she'd let you come on the expedition," Ben said reasonably.

"But what happens when we're out in the Wilderness and we're attacked by monsters and I'm supposed to fight them off?" screamed Barmy. "What happens then? And what happens when Facecrusher wants me to work magic and witchcraft and sorcery and voodoo and the only thing I can come up with is the three card trick? She'll kill me, Ben – you know she will!"

"It's a problem all right, Barmy," Ben agreed.

Ten

"This dwarf," said the Reverend Lancelot Bong cautiously, "his name wasn't Ben, by any chance?"

"Yes," Barmy said, surprised. "Yes, it was."

"Thought so!" exclaimed the Bong triumphantly. "That sort of mess has Ben written all over it."

"You know him then?"

"Old friends," said the Reverend Bong. "Old friends. Went on expeditions together in my younger days. He was very good at getting people into trouble even then." He sniffed. "Thing is, what are we going to do about it?"

"Maybe I shouldn't go on the expedition," Barmy suggested.

"Of course you should go!" The Reverend Bong snapped. "If Kendar's in the Pileggi Mountains, it's the only way you'll get within a hundred miles of him. You're safer with Facecrusher than any other leader I know, so you'd better go on this expedition. The only trouble is Ben's got you in under false pretences. We have to work out what to do about that." He began pacing up and down the room. Above the mantelpiece was the crest of the Church Militant, surmounting the ornately lettered motto, Bless 'em, bash 'em, hack 'em, slash 'em.

Barmy watched him silently. He had been feeling distinctly nervous since his meeting with Facecrusher. Bad enough to be trapped in a different reality. Bad enough to face the Wilderness in a monster-thumping party. Bad enough to have to search a mountain chain for the only man who might, or might not, know how to get you home. But to do it all with a ready-made – and utterly

46

undeserved – reputation as a fighter and magician hardly bore thinking about. To his horror, he found himself half wishing Lauren was here: she'd sort it all out.

"The real problem is the magic business," the Reverend Bong said thoughtfully. "Anybody can bluff their way as a fighter – "

"Excuse me, sir," Barmy said.

But the Reverend Bong was not listening. " – but magic's a different kettle of fish. You can either work it or you can't. I could teach you a bit – healing and so forth: it's part of my priestly skills – but that's not what you want. You need attack spells – flamestrikes, lightning bolts, thundercrushes, that sort of thing. Magical mayhem, what? Not my line at all, except accidentally. When is this expedition scheduled to set out?"

"Day after tomorrow," Barmy said. "Or possibly the day after that: I'm not sure. Look, sir, I don't really think I should – "

"I have an idea," said the Reverend Bong. "Time's a bit tight, but we might just manage it. You come with me."

Barmy bird-dogged the Reverend Bong with a distinct feeling of déjà vu. He seemed to be spending his life walking after peculiar people who were going to sort out his problems and somehow only left them worse. But at least the route was a little less seedy than the one Ben had taken and the destination was not a shop that sold you mummy dust.

They stopped in front of an impressive edifice with steps leading to a door flanked by fluted stone columns. The door was guarded by four burly soldiers wearing chain mail and carrying spears. Barmy eyed them nervously, but they snapped to attention at the sight of the Reverend Bong, who raised one hand beneficently in their direction.

"Bless 'em!" intoned the Bong.

"Bash 'em!" growled the soldiers in unison.

"Hack 'em!" chanted the Bong.

"Slash 'em!" roared the soldiers.

After which the Reverend Bong and Barmy went inside to find themselves in a large paved vestibule with a multitude of doors opening off it and several marble statues set around the walls.

"Excuse me, sir," said Barmy, "but where are we?"

"Town Hall," said the Bong. "I want a word with the mayor. You stay here – I won't be more than a minute."

In fact he was more than ten. For want of anything better to do, Barmy examined the statues and discovered to his surprise that one was of the fat man who had bustled onto the scene after the slith demolished the market square. An inscription on the plinth identified him as the mayor. He looked thinner and more dignified as a statue, but not much.

After a time, the Reverend Bong reappeared, flanked by two men at arms. For a moment, Barmy thought he'd been arrested, but he stepped out as confidently as ever, signalling Barmy to follow as he passed.

"Who are the heavies?" Barmy whispered as he fell in step.

"Guards," said the Reverend Bong in a voice that reverberated through the hall. "They're taking us to jail."

The earlier suspicion returned like a neaptide. "What have we done?"

The Reverend Bong frowned. "What?"

"What have we done?" Barmy repeated. "What have we done that they're taking us to jail."

"Nothing," said the Bong, bewildered. His expression made it obvious he thought he was dealing with a lunatic.

Barmy kept quiet as they marched along a corridor and down several flights of steps. It was obvious they were

48

headed not just for jail but for a dungeon. They had descended sufficiently far to convince him they must now be underground. They reached a cell block. Door after metal-banded door stretched ahead, each one set with a little barred window. Although it was a little high for him, Barmy managed to catch a glimpse through the nearest of them. The cell beyond was no more than three metres square, dripping damp from the walls and furnished only with a heap of filthy straw for bedding. The only thing going for it really was that it was empty. Barmy shuddered. He could imagine being confined in a place like that. What he could not imagine was surviving it for long.

"What have we *done*!" the Reverend Bong said suddenly and began to laugh. "What have we *done* – I see what you mean now. What have we done – nothing. Nothing at all. I'm a member of the Church Militant . . ."

"Bless 'em, bash 'em, hack 'em, slash 'em!" chanted the guards in unison.

". . . so what I do doesn't count. No, dear boy, they're not putting us in jail. Not at all, not even for a short time. On the contrary, we're here to get somebody out."

"Why would we be doing that?" asked Barmy, although a sinking feeling in his stomach suggested he already knew.

"Ah-ha," said the Bong mysteriously.

They turned a corner, marched down another corridor, then halted before a door to a great fussy stamping of feet by the guards.

"Here we are, sir!" one said to the Bong, producing a metallic ring of keys. "Shall I release him now?"

"Yes. Yes, you do that. Stand back, Barmy, this felon may be dangerous."

"It's somebody to teach me magic, isn't it?" asked Barmy gloomily. He knew with certainty that this was the beginning of a major disaster.

"Right!" said the Reverend Bong delightedly. "Right! Bright spark like you will pick it up in no time. Well, you'll have to, won't you, since you're heading out in a couple of days."

The cell door swung open. "All right you – out you come!" ordered the guard.

Barmy did not have to look, did not want to look, but looked anyway. Out of the darkness, blinking a little, emerged the Amazing Presto.

Eleven

Barmy was aware of a staccato clicking noise deep inside his head in the region of his left ear. He was also beginning to see coloured sparkles which danced like fireflies across the turrets and the rooftops of the Keep.

"Breathe!" said the Amazing Presto.

Barmy breathed. *In*, two, three, four . . . *Hold*, two, three, four . . . *Out*, two, three, four . . . *In*, two, three . . . The fireflies changed colour, edging more towards the violet end of the spectrum. The clicking noise inside his head speeded up, like a woman running in stiletto heels.

"Chant!" urged the Amazing Presto.

Barmy chanted. He had a light voice, which the Amazing Presto had been urging him to deepen, but did his best. Since he was learning a very basic spell – one of the five-finger exercises of magic, his mentor called it – the chant was not particularly complicated. It consisted simply of the word (or possibly words) Hub-ya. The problem was it had to be chanted in a sequence of seven repetitions, each one at least slightly different to those which had gone before.

"*Hub*-ya," Barmy chanted. "Hub-*ya*. Hub – " (High pitched) " – ya. Hub – " (Low pitched and gravelly, like Harkaan the Armourer) " – ya. Huuuub-ya. Hub-yaaaaaaaaaaaa. Huuuuuuub-yaaaaaaaa!"

"Gesture!" ordered the Amazing Presto.

Barmy gestured, a delicate, flowing movement similar in many respects to the t'ai chi exercises performed by the entire population of China before breakfast. Barmy's

51

gesture, however, did not take in the whole body, but only his right arm (and to a certain extent his head). It ended in a stabbing movement, two fingers extended, towards a dark green bottle set up as a target some ten metres away across the common.

"Stamp!" screamed the Amazing Presto excitedly.

Barmy stamped his right foot with all the enthusiastic deliberation of a sumo wrestler getting in position.

"Discharge!" howled the Amazing Presto.

"*Eeeeeee-yah!*" yelled Barmy, forcing his concentration to cascade along his arm and rush out through his pointed fingers in the direction of the bottle. A ball of delicate green light appeared quite close to his outstretched hand, crawled forward a few centimetres, then plopped to the ground to fizzle out weakly in the grass. It was pathetic.

Barmy stopped the stupid 4/4 breathing. "It's no good – I'll never get the hang of it. Not in time, anyway."

"But you're almost there, dear boy!" the Amazing Presto exclaimed effusively. "Your progress has been little short of miraculous, although naturally my own teaching may have had something to do with that. Now watch me do it – "

He adopted a dramatic stance, intoned *Hub-ya, hub-ya, hub-ya, hub-ya, hub-ya, hub-ya, hub-ya* without any difference that Barmy could discern, then flung out his hand. A bolt of crackling green energy in the shape of an arrowhead leaped forward missing the bottle by several metres and imbedded itself in the trunk of a nearby oak-tree. The tree split with a crack like overhead thunder, then slowly toppled to demolish a small gazebo, bench and fountain.

"That's the way to do it!" said the Amazing Presto, not at all put out.

Hardly, Barmy thought; but being a placid individual said nothing and started to try again, mainly to head off another of Presto's lethal demonstrations. He breathed, chanted, pointed, concentrated and yelled; and this time a beam of light flickered like a laser from his fingertips, crackling and hissing in a most satisfactory manner. It didn't last long and it missed the target, but it was still a sight better than anything he'd done before.

Barmy stood blinking in pleased amazement. A wide smile washed across the face of the Amazing Presto. "Did I not say that you had talent?"

Although the laser-like beam was impressive for someone who had never studied magic in his life – or even really believed in it for that matter – Barmy knew it was not exactly going to tip the balance against vampires, ghouls, giant weasels or even a run-of-the-mill wolf or two. However much progress he might have made, however pleased Presto might be with him, the simple fact was he did not have the time to turn himself into a fully fledged wizard – or even a reasonably gifted amateur.

He opened his mouth to try to talk sense into Presto when he noticed two figures approaching from the direction of the Keep and shut it again. Even though they were too far away for him to make out their features, the Mutt and Jeff contrast was unmistakable. It was the Reverend Lancelot Bong accompanied by a dwarf who could be only Ben.

Presto caught sight of them as well. "Quickly," he urged, "another go!" He grinned brightly. "You'll impress them this time!"

"I don't see how," Barmy muttered, nevertheless taking up the stance, falling into the 4/4 breathing pattern and beginning a mumbled chant.

"Because I'll give you a little help!" said the Amazing Presto excitedly.

Barmy chilled. "No, Presto, please don't do that! Just leave – "

But it was already too late. "Grondle gohmat gottlo gear . . ." Presto was muttering without moving his lips. "Gehar dejon agat kengo."

A curious sensation engulfed Barmy, as if his mind had been embraced from behind by a polar bear. The fireflies dancing on the rooftops coalesced into shimmering sheets of violet light which set up a high-pitched humming in his head. His right arm began a twitch which degenerated rapidly into an utterly uncontrollable jerking of his entire upper body. He could feel streams of liquid energy coursing up and down his legs.

"Presto!" he shouted desperately.

"Gungum quango rottel luga!" Presto said, eyes pressed tight shut.

Something large, blue-green and spinning began to emerge out of thin air a metre or so from Barmy's outstretched but twitching hand. For one horrific instant he thought it was a slith, but then it resolved itself into a giant, saw-edged, boomerang-shaped blade which took off like a bat out of hell in the direction of Lancelot and Ben. Presto's eyes flicked open. "You're supposed to control where it goes!" he shrieked.

With a whoosh like a guided missile, the huge blade bore down on the approaching figures, who must have seen it since they stopped abruptly. Given its present angle of approach, it would give Ben a haircut and chop the Reverend Bong in two.

"Think where to send it!" Presto screamed. "Stop thinking about those two, Barmy, and think where you want the blade to go!"

Barmy was paralysed. He watched, wide-eyed, as the blade gathered even greater speed and changed inclination so that, on contact, it must decapitate Ben. It set up a howling humming sound as it cut through the air.

"Barmy!" shouted Presto, his face purple.

54

The paralysis broke. With a monumental effort, Barmy wrenched his mind away from his approaching friends and firmly visualized the bottle. For a moment nothing happened, then the whirling blade swung in a shallow arc, accellerated rapidly and swooped to smash the bottle into fragments before popping into nothingness. At once a leprous white humanoid shape sprang up from the debris, prancing and gibbering in a most alarming manner. It looked almost exactly like the thing Fergo Franklin had described: thin, fanged, near-nude and horrible.

"Good grief!" Presto exclaimed. "There was a wraith in the bottle!"

"What should we do?" asked Barmy, almost too numb with surprise to feel afraid.

"Run!" said Presto.

But before he could take this excellent advice, the squat figure of Ben had placed itself squarely in the path of the gibbering wraith, sword drawn, while the Reverend Bong was loping towards it from the back, tugging the mace from his belt.

"Run!" screamed Presto again. "They'll never stop a wraith!"

Barmy did indeed start to run, but towards the creature. Frightened though he was, he felt responsible and had no intention of leaving his two friends to fend for themselves in the emergency.

"Gibber!" went the wraith. "Gibber, gibber!" It raised two skinny arms above its head and hurled itself on Ben.

Barmy crashed into the melee, beating the wraith furiously with his fists and kicking with his feet. "You leave my friend alone!" he screamed. He did little enough damage, but the element of surprise caused the wraith to turn away from Ben. Pink eyes locked on Barmy. "Gibber!" it said, drawing thin lips back to expose more of its glistening fangs.

"Tally-ho!" called the Reverend Bong deliberately as he brought his mace down on the wraith's skull from behind. "Bless 'em, bash 'em, hack 'em, slash 'em!"

The wraith's eyes glazed as its skull caved in. The entire body of the creature began to liquify so that it dissolved into an evil-smelling pool of slime which turned the grass yellow as it soaked into the ground.

"Are you all right, Barmy?" Ben asked as he carefully cleaned off his sword before slowly returning it to the scabbard.

"I think so," Barmy said, heart pounding. It was the first time he had actually attacked *anything*, let alone a wraith, and his emotions were in a bit of a whirl.

"I enjoyed that!" said the Bong. "Just like old times, eh Ben?"

"That's right, Lancie," Ben said. He took a step forward and placed one arm around Barmy's shoulder. "That was very brave of you," he said.

Twelve

The Reverend Bong had brought sandwiches and shared them out with a gusto which suggested the encounter with the wraith had sharpened his appetite. Barmy bit into his and found it contained a tangy mixture of chopped cucumber and pickled beetroot on a lettuce bed. Ben ate solidly. There was no sign of the Amazing Presto, who seemed to have run off shortly after the wraith appeared.

"Now," said the Bong briskly, "the expedition moves out at dawn tomorrow. How's the magic getting on?"

Barmy hesitated. He was, he recognized, a mass of writhing contradictions. The thought of the expedition scared him witless, partly because it meant going back into the Wilderness, partly because Facecrusher terrified him and partly because if the rest of the members were anything like Ben, it would be trouble from the word go. As against all that, he badly wanted to go home and the expedition seemed to be his only chance of finding the alchemist Kendar. And besides, behind the fear, the thought of the adventure excited him.

But it wasn't just a question of whether he wanted to go or not. Ben's little speech to Facecrusher had sunk him without trace unless he could deliver magic – and he doubted that a small green ball of light that travelled a few centimetres (or even a brief, crackling laser beam) was going to do the trick. Of course, if he pretended he was doing better at the magic than he was, they would probably never question it and he might get lucky and never have to prove himself. On the other hand, if he did

57

have to prove himself, he was in big trouble . . . and so, in all probability, were the rest of the party.

He bobbed his head, swallowed hard and decided on the truth. "Not very well," he told the Bong. "The Amazing Presto thinks I've talent, but I know I'm not going to be anything like ready by tomorrow morning."

"Can you work any spell, Barmy?" Ben asked.

"Not really," Barmy admitted.

The Reverend Bong finished his sandwich and wiped some crumbs off his doublet. "Well, it was worth a try," he said. "But not to worry – we'll just switch to Plan B."

"Plan B?" Barmy echoed. He hadn't even been aware they were operating on Plan A.

"Right!" said the Bong. "What I have in mind – "

He was interrupted by the approach of a familiar figure. "Has it gone?" asked the Amazing Presto, glancing hither and yon.

"Hello, Amazing," Ben said. "Yes. Lancie bashed it with his mace."

"I went to check my wraith dispelling spell," Presto explained.

"No you didn't," Ben said. "You ran away because you were chicken."

"And also in order to find some assistance," Presto went on.

"Lucky Barmy wasn't chicken like you," Ben said, "otherwise, I'd have been fanged."

"That's quite enough from both of you," the Bong put in. "Have your argument some other time. Just now I'm quite pleased Presto has reappeared since what I have to say concerns him in some measure."

"Have a sandwich, Amazing," Ben offered. Presto ignored him.

"I gather from Barmy that he won't be ready by the morning – "

"Ready?" The Amazing Presto frowned and shrugged. "Ready? It depends what you mean by ready. He has talent, no doubt at all about that. And he has the best tuition available in the country, from my humble self, that is. And there is still time – "

"Stuff a sock in, Presto," Ben said rudely. "We both know what I mean by ready. He's not going to turn into a fully-fledged war wizard between now and sunrise."

"No . . ." Presto admitted cautiously, ". . . not a fully-fledged – "

"So we're moving to Plan B," said Bong.

"Plan B?" asked Presto, as Barmy had done earlier, but with considerably more alarm.

"What we have," said the Bong, "is a series of needs. What Barmy needs is to get off home for tea and for that he needs Kendar the alchemist and for that he needs to get to the Pileggi Mountains and for that he needs an expedition. What the expedition needs is a war wizard. And a priest, come to that, since I gather Facecrusher's having trouble finding one – "

"They won't go with her, Lancie," Ben put in, "on account of the violent nature of her expeditions."

This was something new to Barmy. "What violent nature?" he whispered to Ben.

"On her last three expeditions, she was the only one to come home," Ben whispered back.

"Dead?"

"Or horribly mutilated," Ben said.

Barmy lapsed into gloomy silence.

"What I'm proposing," continued the Bong, "is that Barmy goes ahead and joins the expedition, even if he can't do much in the way of magic at this stage, but that you, Presto, join with him so you can continue to show him the ropes. That way, Barmy gets to see the Pileggi mountains and the expedition gets a wizard of proven destructive abilities."

The Amazing Presto coughed. "I'm afraid my joining the expedition is quite out of the qu – "

"I didn't mention your need, Presto," Bong said quietly. "Your need is to keep out of prison and I can't think of any other way you're going to manage it." He looked around brightly. "All agreed? No questions? Everybody happy?" When nobody replied, he stood up. "I suggest we all get a good night's sleep tonight – we have an early start in the morning."

"We?" asked Barmy, who missed very little.

"Didn't I mention it?" the Bong said cheerfully. "I'm going with you as the expedition priest."

Thirteen

*Clank . . . clank, clank, clank . . . clank . . . squeak . . .
clank, clank . . .*

The sound of Lancelot Bong's plate armour, a little
rusty here and there, reverberated through the empty
streets. To make matters worse, the Reverend Bong was
singing a jaunty ballad about slaying ghouls. Curtains
twitched as they passed and the occasional shutter opened
on the upper storeys. Barmy skulked along several paces
behind, trying to look as if he was not with him.

"Come along, Barmy!" the Bong called cheerfully.
"This is a big day for you – your first adventure. Never
know what you'll end up to your credit. Wraith, ghoul,
werewolf – maybe even a vampire or two!"

"I just want to get home," Barmy said.

"That too," said the Bong.

They walked through a tunnel and emerged into the
broad courtyard where Barmy had first entered the Keep.
In contrast with the remainder of the sleeping town, here
was all activity. The huge figure of Facecrusher, breastplate glinting from beneath her cardigan, shield strapped
on her back, a massive broadsword at her hip, was
shouting orders to a group of scurrying servants who were
packing supplies onto three patient donkeys.

"Morning, Facecrusher!" Bong called cheerfully.

"Morning, Your Holiness. Good morning, Barmy –
your armour and weapons are over there." She pointed
to a jumbled pile in the care of a Keep guard.

Barmy went across, wondering if insanity ran in his
family or if his present lunacy was a recent development.

He scrabbled through the pile until he found the chain mail which had belonged to Acto the Unlucky and struggled with the unfamiliar fastenings as he put it on. While he did so, his eyes flickered over the remainder of the party.

Ben was over by the gate, dressed in his leather armour, armed with his familiar sword, but now lovingly polishing up the ornate crossbow he had been admiring at the store of Harkaan the Armourer. He looked extremely pleased with himself.

Beside him, striking an heroic pose, was an extraordinarily handsome young man wearing brand-new glistening plate. The morning sun caught the flowing locks of his blond hair, turning it to gold. He held himself very upright, fine chin tilted at a perfect angle, clear, blue eyes focused on the middle distance, as if contemplating such opportunities for decency and courage as the future might contain. This had to be Pendragon and Barmy thought he looked a total twit.

Behind the donkeys, the Amazing Presto was pacing nervously. If he had armour, it was concealed under a flowing robe of pure white linen embroidered with stars, rings and other mystic symbols. He was wearing a pointed hat on his pointed head and carried a stout staff beautifully carved with a wolf's head at one end.

Seated on a backpack a little way from the bustling Facecrusher was a lightly-built man in a leather doublet, the only member of the party who appeared to be totally unarmed. He had an open, innocent, cheerful face and bright, trusting eyes. Barmy wondered if he could be Rowan. He didn't look at all like a thief, but Barmy could not think who else he might be.

Barmy managed the last of the fastenings and straightened up carefully. To his considerable surprise, the armour felt quite comfortable, flexible and warm. It made

62

a funny metallic hissing noise when he moved, but not very loudly and he imagined he would soon get used to it. He rummaged in the heap again until he found his sword (and who would ever have thought Barmy Jeffers would one day, own a sword?). He hefted it to test the weight and found it exceptionally well balanced. In a moment of fantasy, he slashed and stabbed the air, carefully carving up an imaginary orc. As he did so, the astonishing similarity between his present situation and a typical *D & D* adventure suddenly occurred to him. Off to the Wilderness to slay monsters and hunt for gold . . . armed and armoured adventurers . . . even the composition of the party was quite similar to what he had been used to in the *D & D* head-games: fighters, magic user, cleric, thief. Not for the first time he wondered if he might be asleep and dreaming. Or possibly hallucinating, his mind finally driven over the edge by the emotional pressure of living with a sister like Lauren.

Facecrusher moved and Barmy's heart seized up. Behind her was the loveliest girl he had ever seen in his entire life, lovelier even than Queen Nefertiti. She had long, fair hair and steady, clear blue eyes, features like a film star, the smile of a goddess, radiantly healthy golden skin and long slim legs, a lot of which were showing under her short linen tunic. Like Presto, she wore no armour, but strapped to her back was a most peculiar weapon – a large stone ball attached to a metal chain in turn attached to a short handle. The whole thing seemed far too large to handle comfortably, but she was carrying it as if it weighed nothing at all. In so far as he could judge, she was about his own age or just a little older.

"That's Aspen," a familiar voice said at his ear.

He dragged his eyes away. "What?"

"That's Aspen," repeated Ben, who had abandoned his

new crossbow to the packers and come across. "Would you like to meet her?"

"Yes." Barmy gripped his arm. "Yes. Yes, I would, Ben. Yes. Yes, I'd like to meet her. Do you know her, Ben? Can I meet her now, Ben?"

He felt himself tripping over his feet as they walked across, but could do nothing about it.

"Hello, Aspen," Ben said. "I'd like you to meet my friend Barmy. He is young, but he is a lethal fighting machine capable of disembowelling a dragon with his bare hands. Furthermore, he is skilled in sorcery, magic, voodoo – "

"You're doing it again!" hissed Barmy.

"Doing what, Barmy?"

"You're – you're – " He gave up and turned desperately to Aspen. "Please don't pay any attention: I'm not a lethal fighting machine and I'm only learning magic – "

Aspen smiled, bathing Barmy in summer sunshine. "It's all right," she said. "Ben always exaggerates. You should hear what he says about me."

"What do you say about her?" Barmy rounded on Ben, ready to defend her to the death.

"Nothing," Ben grinned. "Aspen really is a lethal fighting machine."

"All right you lot – " The interruption rolled across them in Facecrusher's stentorian tones. " – drop your chat and grab your hat: we're moving out!"

Aspen reached across and squeezed Barmy's hand. "I'm really pleased to meet you, Barmy. I hope you enjoy the expedition."

"He will," said Ben, shouldering his backpack. As an afterthought he added, "Unless he's eaten by a ghoul."

Fourteen

Facecrusher proved as tough as Barmy had anticipated. She ruled the party with a rod of iron, brooking no arguments, seeking no opinions, selecting the route decisively. Although the donkeys carried the equipment and provisions, everyone else was on foot – a surprise to Barmy who had vaguely assumed there would be horses. Because of this, the going was slow and Facecrusher insisted on a dawn start each morning, travelling at a steady pace until sunset, with no more than an hour's break at noon for interim sustenance.

After sunset they made camp and everyone was free to pursue their own interests. For the first three days, Barmy was so exhausted when they stopped that the only thing he did was drop down and fall asleep. But thereafter he began gradually to toughen, so that by the fifth day's march he no longer felt as if his muscles were on fire and even found a little extra energy for conversation in the evenings.

Tough though she was, Barmy came to realize Facecrusher was also exceedingly careful. In his first five minutes alone in the Wilderness, Barmy had encountered a wolf pack and a giant weasel. In his first five days with the expedition, they encountered nothing more threatening than a crow. On the third morning he noticed Facecrusher quietly consulting a map, which presumably meant she knew where she was going – and certainly seemed to suggest she knew the safest way to get there.

There was substantial camaraderie on the expedition. Even Presto, usually difficult and stand-offish, seemed prepared to talk if anybody approached him. But the most friendly of them all was Rowan, who sought Barmy out within hours of their initial departure and showed him how to rearrange his backpack. Barmy was still feeling pleased when Ben returned the purse and dagger Rowan had stolen from him.

"He just does it for practice," Ben explained. "Most of the time he gives you the stuff back himself. Eventually."

Barmy's great interest, of course, was Aspen, with whom he fell more deeply in love every passing day. The problem was that while she was perfectly friendly, she did not appear to be falling deeply in love with him.

The most remarkable member of the party was undoubtedly the Reverend Lancelot Bong. On appearances, he must have been nearly twice the age of the next oldest, but his stamina and energy seemed endless. He rose early in the morning, whistling and singing, and tended to stay cheerful and enthusiastic throughout the entire day. Come evening camp, when even the hardened adventurers showed some signs of fatigue, he often volunteered to do the cooking and frequently talked far into the night at anyone prepared to listen. Most of the talk was about past expeditions, of which he seemed to have joined quite a few and many of his stories were so amazing and ghoulish that Barmy found himself developing a considerable credibility gap.

"Did that really happen?" he asked Ben quietly on one occasion after Lancelot described how he had forced himself to eat an entire skeleton in order to defeat something called a Demi-Lych.

"Yes," said Ben. "But it was only the skeleton of a horse."

On the seventh day, just when Barmy was concluding that the dangers of the Wilderness had been greatly exaggerated, they reached the valley of the ruined castle.

He knew something was wrong the minute he entered the area. Up to this point the Wilderness had been much as he remembered it – rugged, desolate, heavily forested. In the valley, however, the very air smelled alien; dank and chill from a perpetual mist that fell just short of becoming an outright fog.

The vegetation looked peculiar too. In place of the familiar oak and fir forests, the rocky scrubland and occasional grassy plains of the Wilderness through which they had been passing, Barmy suddenly found himself surrounded by twisted succulents, great fleshy plants, interspersed by giant ferns, like the backdrop of a science fiction thriller set on Venus. A peculiar loathing arose in him as he examined the succulents. They had no uniform colour. Some were shades of green, but others were brown, grey, lilac, red and even blue. All dropped moisture and several oozed a thick, resinous sap with a sickly sweet perfume.

"All right you lot!" Facecrusher called sharply. "The ground rules have just changed. You follow me in single file. You have weapons at the ready. You do not, repeat not, touch any plant or leave the path for any reason. If you're attacked, you fight. You do not wait for orders from me. Anything comes at you, you go for it first and ask questions afterwards. Understood?"

"Tally-ho!" shouted Lancelot Bong.

To Barmy's secret relief, Ben moved in front of him, immediately behind Pendragon, who was tailing Facecrusher herself. Aspen, who had unslung her curious chained stone, was about seven paces behind, closely followed by Rowan and Presto, with the Bong bringing up the rear. Everyone was walking very cautiously.

"Why can't we touch the plants, Ben?" Barmy asked quietly, more to relieve his nervousness than because he really wanted to know.

"Some of them are man-eaters," Ben said.

Barmy started to giggle, then saw Ben was serious and swallowed hard instead. He wondered if he should ask why they all had to have their weapons ready, but thought better of it. Now they were a few hundred metres into the valley, he could hear sounds in the undergrowth, slithering sounds punctuated by raucous cries and lizard hisses. It was a fair bet he could guess why they had their weapons at the ready.

"Fear not, Aspen!" Pendragon called back from the vanguard. "I am here to protect you."

Aspen said nothing.

The trail twisted and turned, taking them deeper and deeper into the valley, deeper and deeper into the oppressive mist and gloom. As the light level dropped, the noise level increased until it seemed they must be surrounded by a veritable menagerie of unidentified fauna. Yet for all the noise, not one example of the wildlife did Barmy see: it stalked the undergrowth, but kept clear of the path.

They turned a corner. Facecrusher raised one hand. Ben stopped immediately and Barmy, who had not been paying attention, walked into his back. It was only after he disengaged himself that he saw the castle.

It clung to a barren cliff-face, approachable only by a narrow path that in its upper reaches dropped away sheer on one side into a dizzying precipice. The castle itself was constructed from some glassy, jet-black stone which reflected back the liquid look of the valley and seemed to swallow light so that it hung like some bloated, monstrous spider. Even at this distance, Barmy could see portions of the walls had crumbled, adding an air of utmost desolation to what was already a most unappealing sight. As he stared, Barmy concluded he had never laid eyes on a more evil-looking place. It was Frankenstein's castle and Dracula's crypt all rolled into one.

"That's it, you lot," Facecrusher told them cheerfully. "That's where we're going."

Fifteen

They made camp early in the shadow of the cliff. Face-crusher told them it was far too close to sunset to attempt the ascent: even if they made it to the top in one piece, they would have to enter the castle after dark, which did not bear thinking about.

Lancelot cooked up one of his better stews, but Barmy could only pick at it. Across the campfire, Pendragon had removed his armour and was sitting close to Aspen, who looked lovelier than ever in the firelight. Barmy's head started to trot out a stupid series of if onlys. If only he was bigger. If only he was stronger. If only he was braver. If only he was better looking. If only Pendragon would fall down a hole and get eaten by a slith. None of it was useful.

"Don't you want your stew?" Ben had sat down beside him, clutching an enamel bowl and a tin mug.

"I'm not very hungry."

"I prefer sausages," Ben said. "I can eat a lot of sausages." He dug into the enamel bowl with a fork and speared a chunky bit of carrot. "I wish this was a sausage," he said, examining it carefully. Then he ate it.

They sat in silence except for the sound of Ben savaging his stew. After a while, Ben said, "Are you afraid of what's going to happen tomorrow?"

Barmy nodded. "A bit."

"It won't be so bad, Barmy. Not in daylight. Most of the really nasty things only come out after dark. Unless you go into cellars, of course. That's why Facecrusher's waiting until morning. With a bit of luck, we should be

70

in, grab the loot, and out again by lunchtime. Maybe I'll ask Lancie to do us sausages for lunch."

"It's not just the castle," Barmy said.

Ben finished his stew and set the bowl down, then cupped his hands around the metal mug as he stared into the campfire. "I was married once," he said.

"Pardon?"

"I got married to a girl with green eyes. She was very good-looking and taller than me and the day I met her was the same day her father arranged her betrothal to a Manganian Prince. You wouldn't think someone like me would stand a chance in that sort of situation, but she liked me. It took three years and her father wasn't pleased and the Prince wasn't pleased, but she married me. Her name was Sheena. We were very happy. You have to have patience, Barmy. Patience and hope."

Barmy stared at him, slack-jawed. Eventually he asked quietly, "What happened, Ben?" But Ben's eyes were liquid and he only turned away.

Barmy had trouble sleeping that night. Since the weather was dry, the party stretched out wherever they could find a comfortable spot for their bedding near the campfire. Usually Barmy went out like a light, but tonight he couldn't switch his head off. To make matters worse, the Reverend Bong had taken the first watch and his armour clanked and squeaked as he made his rounds. In a state of mind approaching desperation, Barmy began to imagine himself tackling the castle in a grey fog of total exhaustion.

He was changing position for the eighty-second time when the attack came.

The first he knew about it was a sudden thump and a muffled "What?" from Lancie. He rolled and sat up in one movement. Lancie was upright, threshing around wildly with something thin and grey and not quite human

71

clinging to his back. His visor was up and the creature's arm covered his mouth so that he could not cry out. Another of the creatures, squatting, was embracing an armoured leg. Two more emerged from the undergrowth, half-crouched, sniffing the air, lips flicking back in sound-less snarls like leprous, bald baboons.

Without thought, Barmy grabbed his sword and hurled himself forward. With more experience, he might have yelled a warning to the others, but in the excitement, it never occurred to him. He swung the weapon with more force than skill at the horror wrapped round Lancie's back. The sword bit deep. The creature screamed and dropped away.

"Ghouls!" roared Lancie. "Up and at 'em – tally-ho!" He drew his mace and cracked it sharply on the pate of the thing clinging to his leg. "Bless 'em, bash 'em, hack 'em, slash 'em!"

The others were waking, but slowly, as if drugged by the corrupt night scents of the plants all around them. More ghouls were loping into the clearing. Barmy, who had removed his armour before he lay down and was wearing only a shirt and breeches, felt hands pawing at him from behind. He spun round and lashed out in panic. A horrid face snapped close to his own, then fell away.

"What-ho!" exclaimed the Reverend Bong, leaping about like a lunatic and cracking skulls the while.

Another ghoul jumped straight at Barmy, impaling itself on his outstretched sword. For an instant he was only aware of foetid breath and snapping fangs, then the eyes of the creature glazed and it fell away convulsively, dragging the sword from his hand.

"GHOOOUUULLLLLS!" This from Facecrusher, now fully awake and laying about with her broadsword to considerable effect.

Barmy moved to regain his sword then froze as another

of the horrors, larger than the rest, dropped in front of him, snarling hideously. For a moment, time stood still. With the first flush of excitement gone, Barmy felt a deep chill of raw terror in his vitals. Even with a weapon he would not have given too much for his chances against a thing like this. Without one he was helpless. He dropped back a step. The ghoul's mouth opened, showing mandrill fangs. A grey-white tongue flicked out. It was actually slavering.

Barmy, who was not normally a religious person, began to pray. He raced quickly through the usual promises to become a better human being, got down to the real job of begging for some supernatural escape and had just reached the really desperate bit where he was on the point of undertaking never to annoy his sister Lauren for the remainder of her natural life, when the ghoul sprang.

There was an instant of pure horror: a grey-white face centimetres from his own, fangs bared to tear his throat, clawed hands reaching for his unarmoured body, no escape, no retreat, no opportunity to fight . . .

He closed his eyes. The ghoul's body slammed into his own. He waited for the fangs, then, when nothing happened, opened his eyes again in time to see the creature sliding glassy-eyed into a heap on the ground. It had a metal bolt driven through the base of its skull to protrude immediately below the jaw at the front. In the distance, Ben lowered the ornate crossbow and waved.

Barmy jumped forward and tugged his sword free from the body of the other ghoul, then turned and ran screaming towards a three-strong group of the creatures near the campfire. His earlier terror had drained away to be replaced by a near-insane excitement. He felt – stupidly – he could not be killed.

"Bless 'em, bash 'em, hack 'em, slash 'em!" Barmy yelled as he fell upon the ghouls.

"Go it, Barmy!" called the Reverend Lancelot encouragingly.

The next ten minutes blurred in Barmy's mind. Suddenly all was silence . . .

Panting, Barmy looked around. Close on a dozen ghoul bodies lay strewn about the clearing: the remainder of the creatures had fled. Rowan was standing near him, half leaning on a bloody short sword. The broad figure of Facecrusher was silhouetted against the campfire. Across the way were Ben and Lancie, arms around each other. Barmy felt himself grinning like an idiot.

In the aftermath, it was several minutes before anyone discovered Aspen was missing.

Sixteen

"We must rescue her, of course," Pendragon said. "And quickly. There is not a moment to lose. They will have taken her to the castle, possibly as food for the little ghouls, so we must mount an immediate attack – "

"No," Facecrusher said.

"Pardon?"

"No," Facecrusher said again. "What we've just gone through was a vicar's tea party compared to what we'd face if we entered the castle at night. Not just ghouls either – there are things in there that are much worse. Mounting a night attack would be suicide, utter suicide. We wait for dawn."

"But she could be dead by dawn!" Pendragon protested.

"Very likely," said Facecrusher sourly.

"Isn't there some other way?" Lancelot Bong asked. "Dammit, I like Aspen. We can't just leave her in the hands of those things for the rest of the night."

Facecrusher was deceptively polite. "What do you suggest, Your Holiness?"

Lancie lapsed into a thoughtful silence.

"Perhaps if I went alone . . ." Pendragon offered. "One warrior, unencumbered, under cover of the darkness, creeping with silent stealth into – "

"You wouldn't get ten metres," Facecrusher told him.

"Oh," Pendragon said.

"Just a minute, Facecrusher," Lancelot Bong put in, "maybe there's something in what he says."

"We wouldn't make it as a group and we wouldn't

make it as individuals," Facecrusher said. "There's a trick to surviving in the Wilderness. It's very simple, and I've used it for years to keep expeditions safe. The trick is you stay put at night and watch your back. That's it. I want Aspen back as much as the rest of you, but we're not going to do her any good by running up there like a bunch of amateurs and getting ourselves killed."

"The thing is," Lancelot said quietly, "getting herself killed is almost certainly what Aspen's doing at the moment."

Facecrusher rounded on him angrily. "Think I don't know? This is my fifteenth expedition. *Fifteenth*. I know what happens out here – especially at night. I know what ghouls can do to you – and ghouls aren't the worst things up there. But let me tell you this, Your Holiness, everybody who comes on an expedition takes their chances."

"Facecru – " the Reverend Bong began.

But she had not finished. Her eyes opened and her face rearranged itself into its usual granite mask. "Maybe," she said, "this time Aspen won't make it. It's not certain – she's young, but she's smart and she's quite a fighter. Now this is going to sound hard to you, Your Holiness, but I'm leader of this expedition and I'm responsible for everybody in it, not just for one. The way I see it, if we have lost Aspen, the important thing now is to make sure we don't lose anybody else."

Silence descended like a leaden cloud. After a moment, Ben said, "I have an idea. I was wondering if we could use magic."

All heads turned towards the Amazing Presto, who had exhibited an exceptional sensitivity to the valley's narcotic scents and slept through most of the attack. He was fully awake now, though.

Presto stared ahead blankly for a moment, then said, "Invisibility."

76

"Invisibility?"

"It's tricky," Presto continued, "and there's a certain risk factor, but I think I might manage it. If I made the fighting group invisible they might manage to – "

"Won't work," Facecrusher interrupted. "Most of the things in the castle work on scent as much as sight. They're night creatures. Visible or invisible won't make much difference: you're dead as soon as you go in there."

They lapsed into silence. Presto said thoughtfully, "Attack magic's no good – it's not selective, so it would harm Aspen as much as anything that's got her . . ."

After a while, the little group split up, its members drifting away cocooned in their own thoughts to stretch out and try to sleep before the rescue bid in the morning.

Barmy lay down like the others, but this time he did not even attempt to sleep. He selected a spot in shadow, some distance from the campfire and, when clouds covered the moon, rose again quietly, rolled his bedding to look like a reclining figure, and slipped off into the night.

Seventeen

The path was not so bad. In daylight it would have been a vertiginous nightmare, but at night the sheer drop on the left wasn't visible.

But even though it was a lot less frightening than it could have been, it was still the most frightening thing Barmy had ever done. It was more frightening than his little sister's rages, more frightening than Lugs Brannigan in a foul mood. He fumbled and trembled and shook, listening to the thumping drumbeat of his heart as he edged along, one hand running along the cliff-face to ensure he didn't wander and fall off.

He had his sword in his left hand, his backpack on his back, but the chain mail he'd had to leave behind, fearful that somebody would have noticed had he stayed to put it on. He felt vulnerable without it. His only consolation was that he would have felt just as vulnerable with it. With sword and backpack, he may have looked a little like a *D & D* adventurer, but he certainly did not feel like one. He was fast concluding he was not hero material, whatever his earlier ambitions.

Fortunately he met no ghouls.

The path twisted and turned far more than he had calculated so that there were times when he became so confused he thought he might have wandered off the route completely. It would be just his style: off to rescue a fair maiden and end up lost somewhere in some stupid cave. The memory of the fair maiden spurred him. The thought of Aspen in the hands of those creatures made him sick in his stomach.

There was a light in the castle!

Barmy breathed in so sharply he nearly fell over backwards. Somebody – something – had lit a fire so that the ruins sprang up ahead in stark relief, a ghastly silhouette raised by the flickering flames. A series of rotten thoughts occurred, leading him to an even more rotten conclusion. Ghouls, he knew, ate people – corpses mainly, when they couldn't find anybody fresh. He had assumed they ate them raw, but suppose . . . just suppose . . . Oh Aspen!

Despite his terror, Barmy hurried.

Close to, the castle was far more tumbledown than it had appeared from below. The fire Barmy had seen was burning in an open courtyard, and to his profound relief neither Aspen nor anybody else was roasting over it. He approached with utmost caution, but there was no sign of any ghouls or other nasties. It occurred to him suddenly that if Facecrusher was correct and the castle was infested by creatures of the night they might tend to avoid the area of light around the fire. This thought gave him the confidence to step across the rubble of the west wall into the firelit circle. But he was still plagued by a very nervous thought: who lit the fire?

Now that he was off the treacherous path, he transferred his sword to his right hand, drew a deep breath to stabilize what little courage he had and took a look around.

There was disappointingly little to see. A turret rose up less than twenty metres away, but a turret so broken that it was obviously no more than an empty shell. A tunnel led through into a second courtyard. A further passage gave access to what had once been a substantial portion of the castle, but was now little more than rubble. Close by was an arch, beyond it he could just make out stone steps leading downwards.

Barmy took a torch from his backpack and lit it from the fire. He knew what he had to do and was too frightened to think too much about it.

First he walked through the tunnel to the second courtyard. Several chambers led off it, but when he investigated he found each one empty and their exits blocked. He returned to the first courtyard and checked the tower. As he had suspected, it was no more than a shell. Bats squeaked in the upper reaches, but that was all.

He checked the passage and found, as anticipated, that it ended in a heap of fallen stone. He re-emerged and walked to examine the arch which, as he had seen from a distance, was simply the remnant of some earlier structure and served no useful purpose now.

He blinked, breathed deeply to relieve some of the pressure on his chest and walked towards the steps. There were bones strewn around the approach and he strongly suspected they might be human bones. If there was the slightest comfort to be drawn from the scattering, it was that the only fresh-looking bones were far too large to have come from Aspen, while the remainder were cracked and brown and had obviously lain around for several weeks.

He tried to tell himself this was really good news. Ahead of him, the steps descended into darkness.

Barmy stood on the top step and pushed the torch ahead of him as far as it would go. That proved a fairly serious mistake for a warm wind emerging from the depths blew smoke into his face, triggering a bout of coughing he was helpless to control. He backed off hurriedly. If there was anything within earshot, he had clearly marked his position – not that he was exactly inconspicuous carrying the torch in the first place.

He waited. Nothing emerged from the darkness. A

clear suspicion was growing in his mind that the real dangers of this castle were in its lower reaches. He stifled the thought, waited a little longer, then stepped forward.

The stairs were broad, well worn and strewn with organic litter. He began to descend. As he moved, he listened, straining to catch the slightest sound which would indicate an impending attack. Facecrusher was right: this was lunacy. But he felt he had little choice.

He reached a stone-paved landing and felt his heart stop as something rushed towards him from the darkness. But it was only a rat, large enough to have scared him witless at any other time, but now actually a relief. The creature raced around his foot and disappeared. Barmy crossed the landing and started on the second flight.

The stairs brought him to a stone-slabbed corridor which ended in a wooden door. Branch corridors ran off to his left and right. For a moment he hesitated, desperately uncertain what to do next. All he could think of was rescuing Aspen, not how he was going to manage it. Eventually, lacking any better plan, he moved towards the wooden door. As he did so, ghouls surged in a silent stream from both side corridors and fell upon him.

Eighteen

Barmy came to in a torchlit chamber, embarrassingly dressed only in his jockey shorts (fortunately clean on that morning) and tied to a rectangular block of chocolate-coloured granite which, judging by the hideous image towering over him, served as some sort of altar.

He suffered from a moment of disorientation, not to mention a considerable pounding pain from the blow to the back of the head which had knocked him out. He was having trouble remembering exactly what had happened. He recalled a corridor and what seemed like an army of ghouls, but after that very little except flashes of a fight, but the overall picture was very vague.

He looked around, and saw he was in a massive, high-ceilinged, collonaded chamber, decked in the trappings of a temple. For want of anything better to do, Barmy examined his bonds. There were leather straps around his ankles, chest and wrists and a loose hemp rope around his neck. The set-up allowed him some mobility, but not much; certainly not enough to give him any hope of slipping free. Besides which, if he did slip free, where was he going to go? Even if, miraculously, he could escape the congregation of ghouls, he had not the least idea of where he was. He assumed the temple chamber was somewhere underneath the black ruin, but how to reach the surface he did not know.

Well, he thought bitterly, Facecrusher was dead right. This was suicide. Oddly enough, he did not feel quite so terrified as he imagined he would. Frightened enough, of course, but not so heart-thumpingly, gut-wrenchingly paralysed as he had been when, for example, the rat raced past him on that first landing. It was as if, now that the worst had happened, something in him had relaxed. There was, after all, very little he could do.

He found he regretted his predicament not so much for his own sake as for the fact that Aspen's last hope was gone. Not that it had been much of a hope in the first place, but still . . .

He turned his head to find a small group of robed and hooded figures had entered through a distant door and were moving towards him in solemn procession. Although he could not see their faces, the way they moved suggested these were not ghouls. Besides, most of them were too tall. Superficially, they looked human, like an outing of the Ku Klux Klan which had wandered through a Möbius Warp. But it was unlikely they actually were human. What human could survive down here in the heart of Ghoulsville? Far from attacking, or even threatening, the ghouls had actually drawn back a little, as if afraid.

What sort of creature frightened ghouls?

He noticed the two figures flanking the tall leader were carrying small ceremonial cushions on which rested, respectively, a shallow bowl and a long-bladed, curving, sharp-edged knife.

The hooded figures stopped some two metres from the altar. Their leader raised two arms, "Hail Tanaka!" he intoned in a deep, masculine voice. "Hail Obedniga!"

"Hail Tanaka!" chanted the remaining robed ones. "Hail Obedniga!"

A howling chorus erupted from the ghoul congregation, as if the creatures were trying to emulate the words. The leader allowed the noise to continue for a moment, then lowered his arms. At once a hush fell throughout the chamber.

Moving with great deliberation, the leader turned to

the figure on his right and lifted the curved knife with great reverence from the cushion. He turned with his back to Barmy and raised the knife as if showing it to the congregation.

"With this blade, we sacrifice to Tanaka!"

The howling erupted again and several of the ghouls began to jump up and down on the spot in excitement. Barmy wondered if the last one on the altar had been Aspen.

The hooded figure returned the blade to its cushion, then turned again, holding up the shallow bowl.

"With this vessel we accept the gift of blood to feed Tanaka!"

"Hail Tanaka!"

"Hail Obedniga!"

The hooded figure returned the bowl and took up the knife again, this time rolling back the sleeves of his robe to reveal hairy, but quite human arms. He walked forward until he stood directly over Barmy. Through the slits in the hood, Barmy could see two dark, glittering and, he thought, completely loony eyes.

"Rejoice!" said the figure. "Your spirit has been chosen to serve the great Tanaka!"

"Get lost," Barmy told him rudely, surprised – and rather pleased – by his own nerve. Of course, when you're about to get your throat cut, you don't have a lot to lose. But all the same . . .

If the figure was offended, it did not show. "For this great honour, you will be required to pay the small price of your life's blood, after which your heart will be dispatched to Tanaka as a token of your loyalty."

So that was it then, Barmy thought. Throat slit then the old heart cut out. It didn't leave much to look forward to.

"Hail Tanaka!"

"*Hail Tanaka*"

"Hail Obedniga!"

"*Hail Obedniga!*"

The figure raised the knife, holding it with both hands. The robed figure with the bowl came forward to kneel beside the altar. From the body of the temple, the ghouls began to stamp bare feet in unison. The effect was a rhythmic sound, not unlike drumming.

Nineteen

He was obviously the sort of semi-literate tort-feasor who likes to draw out the agony. But when the knife remained suspended, moment after moment, Barmy's quaking terror was actually replaced (at least in part) by irritation and, incredibly, impatience. Then, to his amazement, the knife dropped: not across his throat or into his thumping heart, but straight down to clatter on the floor.

The hooded figure teetered, swayed, crumpled a little, then pitched forward across Barmy's bound body. Barmy lifted his head slightly, and saw a metal bolt driven through the figure's neck at the base of the skull.

"Ben?" Barmy whispered, scarcely able to believe the evidence of his eyes.

For an instant time froze, then things started happening with ever-increasing speed and finally there was pandemonium.

The first thing Barmy was aware of was the kneeling figure beside him throwing away the sacrificial bowl and drawing a knife every bit as sharp and menacing as that which had just been dropped. Barmy flinched away as the blade flashed towards his throat, but tied as he still was he could do nothing. But the knife did not plunge for a kill. Instead it sliced neatly through the rope around his neck. "Hold still!" the figure hissed.

It was Aspen's voice! Even in his terror and confusion he knew he could not be mistaken. The kneeling figure in the robe and hood was Aspen! He held still: he was too paralysed by shock to move. The knife began to hack through the leather bands at his wrists.

"Aspen?" Barmy said, scarcely able to believe what he knew to be true.

"Yes, it's me, Barmy." With her free hand she pulled off the hood. Blonde hair tumbled down in a golden stream. She grinned at him, eyes alive with excitement.

Barmy was vaguely aware that a second hooded figure had pitched forward with a crossbow bolt in the base of its skull. Only seconds later another joined it, then another and another. Briefly he wondered where Ben had stashed himself to do his poison dwarf act. Wherever he was, he had a good view of the proceedings and an uninterrupted line of fire.

The ghoulish congregation woke up at this point and turned into milling, howling chaos. The creatures were aware of something dreadful happening, but obviously could not quite pinpoint the immediate source of the attack. After a moment, frustration got the better of them and they began to fall upon one another. With the first spurt of blood, their excitement reached a frenzy.

"Bless 'em, bash 'em, hack 'em, slash 'em – Tally-ho!" a familiar voice called out from somewhere in the body of the chamber. The rallying cry was followed almost instantly by a crunching sound that made Barmy wince.

The leather strapping fell away. Barmy sat up shakily, pushing the body of the leading figure off his legs. The scene in the temple defied description. Ghouls were snapping and tearing at ghouls. Hooded figures were screaming, running round in panic and dropping with dreadful inevitability, one after one, from the effects of crossbow bolts in the neck. And in the middle of the maelstrom, a tall, thin figure, robe and hood thrown back to reveal plate armour, was leaping like a dervish, crushing skulls with his mace. As his eyes swept the chamber to take in the scene, Barmy caught sight of Ben seated

87

cross-legged in an ornamental niche high up in one wall.
He was sighting his crossbow on another hooded figure.

Barmy felt the hilt of his sword being pressed into his
hand. "Go get them, Tiger!" Aspen hissed into his ear.
She flung off the restricting robe, vaulted over the altar
and raced towards the fray, swinging her curious stone-
ball weapon as easily as if it were made of polystyrene
foam.

Surprise and shock held Barmy immobile for a second
longer, then suddenly loosened their grip. "Aspen!" he
screamed, suddenly fearful that, having found her again,
he was about to witness her death at the hands of a dozen
snarling ghouls. He slid from the altar block and launched
himself after her in mounting desperation, but tripped
and fell across a body before he had gone three steps.
"Aspen!" he called again, as he picked himself up. He
started forward, then stopped, his capacity for surprise
not yet completely numb.

It was like nothing he had ever seen before, like nothing
he had remotely imagined in the wildest of his heroic
fantasies. Aspen cut a swathe through the ghouls like a
scythe through corn. The huge stone ball actually blurred
and hummed at the end of its chain as she swung it, to
devastating effect. Ghouls were flung against walls,
against pillars. Screams of terror mingled with the snap of
broken bones.

Suddenly, against all reason, she dropped her weapon
on the floor and swung to face a dozen or so remaining
ghouls empty-handed. For an incredulous instant, Barmy
stared, mouth open, then launched himself forward. Two
of the creatures swung round to meet him.

Thunk! To his right another hooded figure pitched
forward sporting a bolt at the base of its skull.

" – hack 'em, slash 'em!" Lancelot called gaily, hitting
heads.

Barmy lunged at an approaching ghoul and more by luck than judgement caught it in the throat. His stroke was not accurate enough to kill, but caused sufficient damage to force it to fall back. He stepped forward to press his advantage, temporarily ignoring the second ghoul – which proved a bad mistake. The first ghoul slipped and dropped down on one knee. Barmy drove towards it and the second ghoul jumped forward to sink a set of slimy fangs deep into the muscles of his shoulder.

Pain seared through him like a white-hot brand. He had once been bitten, quite severely, by a dog. But it was nothing like this. The dog bit and jumped away. The ghoul bit and clung. To his horror, Barmy could actually feel the creature chewing! In a moment of exquisite panic he realized he was being eaten.

Nausea erupted at the thought and for the barest instant he felt his head swim and wondered if he would be so stupid as to faint. Then common sense prevailed and he flung himself backwards with all his strength to crush the ghoul against a nearby pillar. The brute gasped and dropped away, tearing a bit off Barmy's shoulder as it did so. He ignored the pain and whacked it with his sword, then swung back to face the first ghoul which was now scampering towards him on all fours.

Thunk! The last of the robed and hooded figures collapsed.

Barmy slashed at the ghoul which caught his sword blade and clawed along it, wide, feverish eyes locked on the bloody wound at his shoulder. The sight seemed to send it utterly insane, for it made no attempt at all to defend itself as it scrabbled and drooled in a horrifying effort to tear the wound with its fangs. Barmy pushed forward and pierced the chest with his sword, killing it instantly.

A noise behind told him the second ghoul had

recovered and he swung to meet it. Fortunately the creature was staggering, still partly stunned and he dispatched it easily as it leaned towards him. To his left, he could see Aspen moving like a tenth dan black belt in the martial arts, kicking, punching, chopping, snapping necks and arms and backs while not a single ghoul could lay a finger on her.

And this, thought Barmy wryly, was the maiden he had innocently set out to rescue. He was still grinning at the thought when a dreadful weakness, spreading from his shoulder, reached his head to dim his eyes and sent him pitching forward into darkness.

Twenty

His shoulder felt most peculiar: not painful exactly, not even really uncomfortable, but all of a tingle, as if it were full of fizzy drink. The rest of his body – and particularly his head – felt quite peculiar, too. He was no longer weak and there was little indication he was about to pass out again, but he seemed to be lighter somehow, the way he imagined astronauts must feel while walking on the moon. This sensation of lightness was not consistent, but came and went in waves. When they peaked, he seemed about to float away.

Barmy opened his eyes. He knew at once he was no longer in the black castle ruin, no longer even in the ghastly valley. He was in a camp set up in barren flatland, stretched on a litter, lightly bound with straps to stop him falling off.

But what rivetted his attention was the Reverend Lancelot Bong, no more than a metre away. The Bong was devoid of his plate armour – indeed, devoid of all his clothes except a pair of blue and white spotted boxer shorts, leather boots and socks held up by little suspenders. Around him flamed an aura of crackling blue electricity, as if he had just been struck by lightning. His hair was standing on end and his beard bristled outwards like a hedgehog. Both his hands were outstretched with bolts of energy running up and down between them like something Viktor Frankenstein would use to animate his monster. He seemed to be dancing, using precise, high-stepping movements similar to a Scottish sword-dance.

Ranged around this apparition were the other members

of the party, watching with obvious fascination – except for Aspen and Facecrusher, both of whom had their backs turned. The blue energy dimmed and flared by turns while streams of it licked out to curl around the watchers – including Barmy, who was too surprised to try to pull away and yet the fizziness in his shoulder increased.

"He's awake," Ben said, glancing towards him.

"What?" the Bong danced even closer, peering. When he found Barmy's eyes were open, he grinned. "There you are – what? And not a minute too soon – bits of me were getting chilly." The electrical fire died abruptly and the Amazing Presto stepped forward with a robe which he wrapped around the Bong's shoulders.

"You can look now," Ben said. "He's decent."

Facecrusher and Aspen turned at once. Both looked at Barmy, not at the Bong.

"Feeling better?" asked the Bong.

"Yes," Barmy said. "Yes, I am." Which was true. He tried to sit up, failed, then pushed the strapping down and managed it. "Yes," he said again, "I'm feeling very well. What's going on?" His eyes fell on Aspen, whose head was bandaged.

"Lancie was healing you," Ben said.

"What was all the lightning stuff?"

"That's the way he does it."

Growing stronger by the minute, Barmy felt his shoulder where the ghoul had eaten bits. There was no pain, no indication of the slighest wound. Even the fizziness was dying down. To the Reverend Bong he said a little uncertainly, "Thank you. Thank you, sir."

"Don't mention it," the Bong said. He moved off presumably in search of his clothing and armour.

"Are you really all right?" This was from Aspen, who had come over and was now kneeling down beside him.

Barmy flushed. "I think so. What – "

92

"Well," said Ben very loudly, "I'll be leaving you two now because I have important things to do." He stood up and tramped off ostentatiously.

" – happened to your head?" Barmy asked.

"It's nothing really."

"It's bandaged."

"One of the ghouls hit me with a rock."

"Are you badly hurt?"

"No," Aspen shook her head, then winced at the sudden movement. She grinned at herself. "There was a lot of blood at the time, but that's stopped now. It aches a bit, that's all. A couple of days and I'll be good as new."

"Why don't you get the Reverend Bong to heal it the way he did my shoulder?" He felt his old wound site again, marvelling at the cure.

A smile flickered on the edge of Aspen's mouth. "He gets embarrassed healing women – he can't do it unless he takes his clothes off. When he's embarrassed, the energy goes all over the place – like the Amazing Presto on a bad day. It's usually simpler to let time heal you."

"Oh," Barmy said. His mind was still in a bit of a whirl following the recent excitement. "What happened to you, Aspen?" he asked, "I don't mean the wound – I mean from the time the ghouls attacked our camp."

Aspen shrugged. "They caught me asleep – I'm like Presto: the plants have a strong effect on me. They carried me off to the ruins while the rest of you were fighting."

"Why didn't they just kill you on the spot?"

"I suppose they wanted to sacrifice me to Tanaka the way they tried to do to you. I woke up while they were carrying me downstairs. Ghouls are pretty stupid really – they hadn't taken away this . . ." she touched the curious stone-ball weapon still slung over her shoulder. ". . . so what with the weapon and the element of surprise, I was able to do them a certain amount of damage . . ."

"What sort of damage?"

Aspen cast her eyes down demurely. "Like death. There were only half a dozen of them."

Barmy sighed inwardly. He was hard put to hold his own against one ghoul. She was talking blithely of dispatching six. And he was the one who had mounted the rescue mission!

" – avoided the main colony," Aspen was saying, "and came up to the surface. I lit a fire, partly as a signal to Facecrusher, partly to keep anything else away – most of the things up there don't like a lot of light. Then I heard something coming despite the fire and hid. That was you, as it turned out, but by the time I realized that, you'd gone down the steps and got yourself captured."

Barmy closed his eyes in embarrassment. She'd killed her captors, made herself safe – well, reasonably safe – and he'd promptly blundered through to stick his head in the lion's mouth.

"Fortunately, Ben and Lancie turned up almost at once. Ben was actually following you – he'd noticed you creeping off. Lancie had the same notion as you did about rescuing me: he'll use any excuse to get into trouble. At that stage we thought we'd only ghouls to contend with, but it turned out there were Tanaka worshippers up there too – "

He made a mental note to ask her about the Tanaka worshippers. They seemed human, but they had obvious control of the ghouls. For now, however, he just listened, growing more embarrassed by the minute.

" – which actually made things a bit easier, since we were able to steal robes to disguise ourselves." She shrugged again. "You know the rest."

"Yes," Barmy said. He half turned away, too embarrassed now even to look at her.

"Barmy?"

"Yes, Aspen?"

"I want to thank you for trying to rescue me."

Barmy blinked. "You were the one who did the rescuing." He realized he hadn't thanked her and added with utter sincerity, "I'm ever so grateful."

"That's as maybe," Aspen said, "but sometimes it's the thought that counts. You weren't to know I was all right. And there were some people – " Her eyes flickered to the right. Pendragon was seated polishing his shiny armour some distance away. " – who were quite content to sit back and let others take the risks."

"Facecrusher told us we should wait until morning. I mean, I went off because I didn't know any better, but she absolutely insisted we stay put." Why, he wondered, was he defending Pendragon? But his tongue was in gear now and running like a well-oiled engine headed for the cliff. "I'm sure Pend – I'm sure everybody wanted to go up after you right away and Pendragon actually suggested it and there was a long discussion – a very long discussion about magic and the best thing to do and – "

He stopped. Aspen had kissed him.

Twenty-one

A little later, when Barmy had quite recovered, Ben rejoined them.

"Have you told him about Kendar?" he asked Aspen.

"Not yet, Ben."

"I think you should, Aspen. It's very important to Barmy."

"What about Kendar?" Barmy asked, looking from one to the other. He had a sinking feeling this was not going to be good news, but the impact of the kiss remained with him and he did not panic as much as he would have normally.

Aspen licked her lips. "I'm afraid he's not in the Pileggi Mountains, Barmy."

"Which is good news," Ben put in hurriedly. "The Pileggis are huge and riddled with caves. You could spend months and months looking for him there."

"How do you know he's not in the Pileggi Mountains?" Barmy asked, trying to conceal his panic.

"Well – " She licked her lips again, a clear indication of nervousness. " – I told you the Reverend Bong and I got hold of hooded robes to put on . . ."

"Yes." She was stringing it out because she didn't want to tell him. It had to be really bad news.

"Well," said Aspen, "the thing was that one of the characters who didn't need the robes any more was on leave from the Baron's castle and he had some papers on him that mentioned the alchemist Kendar had been captured and taken to the castle. I think they must have taken him before he even reached the Pileggi Mountains."

She scratched the side of her nose. "There was some suggestion Obedniga wanted him."

Who was the Baron? Where was his castle? Obedniga sounded familiar, although he could not quite – yes, he could! *Hail Tanaka! Hail Obedniga!* It was part of the chant when he was being sacrificed. "You're going too fast for me, Aspen," he said carefully. "Who is this Baron?"

"Baron Tanaka," Aspen said.

Barmy blinked. "Baron Tanaka." He stared at her for a moment. "Tanaka is some sort of rotten god they tried to sacrifice me to – that ugly great idol underneath the ruin."

"What?" asked Aspen, obviously confused.

But Ben knew what Barmy meant. "That wasn't an ugly great idol, Barmy," he said soberly. "That was an ugly great statue of the Baron. A very good likeness, too."

"You mean," asked Barmy, appalled, "that thing actually exists?"

"Oh, yes." Ben was nodding up and down like one of those little ornaments with a pendulum head. "That thing actually exists all right. That thing is Baron Tanaka."

"I'm sorry, Barmy," Aspen said. "I thought you knew. Baron Tanaka is the ruler of the Wilderness. He's supposed to be the most evil creature ever born."

"And the most dangerous," Ben put in with a little grin.

"But those people were worshipping him!" Barmy protested. "They were trying to sacrifice me to him!"

Aspen nodded. "That's part of it. Tanaka has been Lord of the Wilderness for more than fifty years. After a while the rumour got about that he was an incarnate god – well, incarnate demon, really – and a cult grew up to worship him. Tanaka encouraged it, of course: it ensured supplies of dedicated, loyal and fanatical followers any time he needed them."

"So Tanaka actually exists – a real living, breathing human being?"

Aspen nodded.

"Who's Obedniga?" Barmy asked.

"The Baron's war witch," Ben told him.

Aspen said, "There's not as much known about her as about the Baron. Actually, nobody had ever heard of her until a very short time ago, although she may have been working secretly for the Baron for years. She seems to be an incredibly powerful sorceress. Rumour has it she's just as evil and even more ruthless than the Baron himself. She supports him in everything he wants to do – they say it's because he's promised she will be ruler of the Wilderness after he dies. She's a lot younger than he is, so it may be worth her while serving him now in exchange for future gains."

"And these two have got Kendar?"

Aspen nodded. "Yes."

"What do they want with him?"

She shrugged. "Who knows? He's an alchemist, so perhaps he's stumbled on some valuable secret."

"Or perhaps they just want to feed him to their ghouls," Ben said, grinning widely this time.

"Ben's only joking, Barmy," Aspen said quickly. "But I have to tell you in all fairness Kendar might not survive for long in the Baron's castle unless he has some ability, something only he can do, and it's important to them, then he could last for years."

"But I have to find Kendar otherwise I'll never get home!" Barmy wailed, suddenly overpowered by his situation.

"We know, Barmy," Ben said kindly. "That's why we're going with you."

Barmy's eyes widened. "We?"

"All of us," Ben said. "Aspen had a word with Face-crusher and she's agreed to back you with the whole expedition."

Twenty-two

At the end of an uneventful second day's march towards Castle Tanaka, Barmy discovered he was rich. With no fights to fight or strategy to plan, Facecrusher had been catching up on the book-keeping and the results came as a bombshell to Barmy. His share amounted to approximately seventy-eight thousand gold pieces.

It seems that while Barmy was unconscious after being bitten by a ghoul, the Bong discovered that only a small contingent of ghouls had been left to man the ruins. The remainder had been transported to Castle Tanaka for defence duty.

With the greater portion of the ghouls now many miles away and the remainder carpeting their temple, the Bong, Aspen and Ben were faced with a unique opportunity to explore a warren safely. They did; and found the original treasure room of the black stone castle.

It contained gold and silver bullion, a vast array of artefacts and artworks and seven bags of gemstones.

Ben was dispatched to convey the news to Facecrusher who led the remainder of the expedition up the path at first light. Even with the pack animals, it was impossible to loot the entire store – there was just too much. So the art and artefacts were ignored, except for a few personal souvenirs, but they took all seven bags of gems and as much gold as the donkeys could comfortably carry.

Even though it was only a small part of the hoard, it represented a vast fortune by any calculation: certainly enough to justify the expedition ten times over. Aspen had later proposed that they use this to finance the expedition to find the alchemist Kendar.

Facecrusher accepted her suggestion without reservation, almost certainly because she enjoyed adventure more than she enjoyed money. Thus the decision to march on Castle Tanaka was taken.

But Barmy only learned all this much later, pieced together from small bits of information gathered here and there. Being rich did not, of course, make a great deal of difference in the short term. They still ate the same rations, still stood the same guard watches, still slept rough and worried about monsters. But it created a warm feeling in the pit of Barmy's stomach that would not go away. He wondered what seventy-eight thousand gold pieces would be worth in his own reality. He thought it had to be a fortune.

When he wasn't dreaming about his money, Barmy was worrying about his problems. He was, he knew, a congenital worrier, but he had never been able to do anything about it. He worried about Aspen, whose head was gradually healing, but who had, it seemed to him, been avoiding him. He worried about where they were going, for while everyone treated the march on Tanaka's castle as routine, he knew it was probably the most deadly dangerous venture an expedition had ever undertaken. He worried about getting home again, for there was, of course, no guarantee that the alchemist Kendar would actually be able to help him.

But most of all, or at least most immediately, he worried about the Amazing Presto.

Barmy's magical training had lapsed almost from the instant the expedition started. At first he had simply been too exhausted. Later, when his body acclimatized to the tough conditions, there always seemed more important things to do. Now, however, all that had changed.

It was Facecrusher who put it in perspective. "We're not going to go in the front door," she said, referring to Castle Tanaka. "And we're not going to go in together. Our only hope is stealth. That means you could find yourself on your own, Barmy. And for somebody your age and size, magic has to be your only real protection."

Barmy took a deep breath. "There's something I have to tell you, Facecrusher – "

"That Ben's a little liar?" Facecrusher asked. "You don't have to tell me that: I've known it for years."

"So you knew I wasn't skilled in magic, sorcery, voodoo – "

"Of course I did. I took you on because you looked a willing lad and Ben was vouching for you. But if you knew no magic then, you'd better learn some before we reach Castle Tanaka. If I were you, I'd have another talk to Presto."

Which he did; and the training resumed.

For some reason it went better than it had done at the Keep. Amazingly, he produced and hurled his first real fireball after only three short lessons. It was not nearly so powerful as the fireballs Presto threw and he felt exhausted afterwards, but it was a fireball and it travelled and it hit its target. After he produced it, he had to lie down for fifteen minutes.

"That's just a beginner's reaction," the Amazing Presto assured him. "A lot of magic works using your personal energy. It can be very tiring until you get used to it."

"But will I be used to it by the time we tackle Baron Tanaka?" Barmy asked, visualizing that terrifying statue in the temple.

"You will if you practise," Presto said.

So Barmy practised. Presto and Facecrusher had agreed

between them that it would be pointless giving Barmy a broad training in the mystic arts. There was no time for that sort of refinement. Instead, the concentration was on three spells: the theory being that if he could master them, they might be enough – just enough – to get him through the dangers ahead.

The first spell was Fireball Firing, which, if it went properly, conjured up a flaming ball of gas that could be mentally directed to hurl itself against a designated enemy. The second was Personal Protection, which created a sort of weak, invisible force-field around Barmy's head and body. The field only lasted twenty minutes, however well the spell was cast, but while it lasted, it made Barmy difficult to hit in battle. Not impossible, the Amazing Presto stressed, but difficult; and if he was hit the chances were he would not be so badly damaged as he would have been without the spell.

The third spell was in a very different category to the other two. Presto insisted he practise the first two time and time again, however bored and tired he felt. The third spell Presto would not permit him to practise at all. Instead, he taught Barmy the words and gestures separately, and the mental disciplines separately again. Only when all three were put together – words, gestures and thought patterns – would the spell actually work . . . if it was going to work at all.

It was, said the Amazing Presto, an advanced spell and horribly dangerous even for experienced magicians. He would not, he said, have dreamed of teaching it to a beginner like Barmy except in an emergency. Where they were going constituted an emergency situation. There was no question of practising with this spell as he had the others and Presto warned Barmy not to use it – not to even think of using it – except as a very last resort. The sort of last resort, stressed Presto, where the

103

only possible alternative was death . . . and perhaps not even then.

Barmy needed little urging on that score. His blood had chilled and stayed chilled since he had heard the title of the spell. Presto called it Summon Slith.

Twenty-three

There was a slight miscalculation in the timing of the march so that they did not catch sight of Castle Tanaka until the evening of the fifth day – which at least had the benefit of giving Barmy a little extra time to practise his magic. The first glimpse, on the distant horizon, showed a brooding fortress holding the high ground like some squat and monstrous spider, its heavy outlines broken here and there by slim, castellated towers and pointed spires.

They camped then, well distant from their goal, and the following morning climbed a ridge which gave them a clear view of the castle and its surrounds. It was like nothing Barmy had ever seen before.

For a moment there was total silence in the party, then Pendragon said, "How do we get in?"

"Underground," Facecrusher told him shortly. She turned and began to walk back down the ridge. "Come on: we need a little conference to discuss tactics."

They sat around the dying embers of the campfire as the sun climbed higher in the sky.

"There's only one way you can reach Tanaka, so far as anybody knows," Facecrusher told them, "and that's by tunnel. There's an entrance passage about two kilometres from here. The tunnel cuts below the lava streams and brings you out at the foot of the rock. From there you climb steps to the entrance gate."

"But isn't it guarded?" asked Pendragon.

"Heavily," Facecrusher said. "There are ghoul patrols and seven security checks – four along the length of the

105

tunnel, one at the foot of the steps, one on the steps and the last one at the castle gate. In the castle, they say Tanaka keeps a standing garrison of ten thousand."

"An army couldn't take that place!" Pendragon breathed.

Although he didn't want to ask it, Barmy asked, "Then how are we going to get in, Facecrusher?"

For the first time her expression softened slightly and she grinned. "By becoming people who are supposed to get in. We take a leaf out of Lancelot and Aspen's book." When he continued to look blank, she added, "We disguise ourselves as Tanaka cultists!"

"Ta-ra!" exclaimed the Bong, leaping up to pull a hooded robe out of a pack on one of the donkeys. He had obviously been in on the plan.

"Are there robes for each of us?" asked the Amazing Presto.

Aspen nodded. "We thought they might come in handy," she said coyly.

"All right," Facecrusher said, "this is where it gets a little nervous. If we go in as a group, we wouldn't get further than the first ghoul patrol. However, if we split up, there's a chance. My plan is that we go in singly at irregular intervals over the day. Normally even this would be highly dangerous, but it's Tanaka's birthday in a week and there are always a lot of pilgrims arriving at this time to pay their respects, so security tends to get overburdened and consequently a little lax. Once you get through the main gate, you'll find there are visitors' facilities before you enter the castle proper. One of these is a smallish tavern. We'll meet up there at sunset. If you're waiting, don't order mead – it's overpriced. Any questions?"

"I don't like it," Pendragon said sourly.

"What's your plan then?" Facecrusher asked.

Pendragon fell silent.

After a while, Barmy asked, "Who goes in first?"

Facecrusher cleared her throat. "I will, but actually there's one more thing: you'll be staying here, Barmy."

"Staying here?"

"You won't be coming into the castle. Nothing personal, but you just don't have the fighting experience for this sort of job." She smiled. "So you can find a nice spot to relax and wait and before you know it, we'll have the alchemist Kendar back out ready to – "

"I'm going," Barmy said.

"Barmy, I just told you – "

"I'm going, Facecrusher," Barmy said again, heart pounding. "It's my problem and even though you're right about my experience, I'm not going to let you take that sort of risk unless I go."

"Barmy, I – "

"If you don't agree, I'll go anyway," Barmy told her bluntly. "I'll wait until you've all gone, then I'll follow you. There's no way you can stop me. It would be too dangerous to leave me tied up out here and what else can you do?"

"He's right, Facecrusher," the Bong said.

For a moment Facecrusher teetered on the edge of anger, but then she said, "Very well, Barmy – that's your choice. But it's a dreadful risk."

"I think Barmy should come with me when I go in," Ben said suddenly. "I don't think two pilgrims together look very much more suspicious than one, especially if the guards think they're both dwarves. And if we go together, I could look after Barmy and Barmy could look after me."

Facecrusher stared at him for a moment, then said, "That's an excellent idea, Ben – we'll do that." She gestured. "Now gather round – I want to tell you a few things you'll need to know to pass as Tanaka cultists."

Both Barmy and Ben were difficult to fit with robes because of their size, but the Amazing Presto proved remarkably adept with a needle and thread, so that before long they had disguises which might have been tailored for them.

Facecrusher was first to leave, tall, broad and quite imposing in robes she had pulled on over breastplate and cardigan. The Bong went next, after three quarters of an hour, then, reluctantly, half an hour later, Pendragon.

A full hour passed before Aspen strode off, looking as lighthearted as a party-goer. Twenty minutes later, the Amazing Presto stood up. "Don't forget those spells," he called over his shoulder to Barmy.

The seconds ticked by, each one an eternity. Face-crusher had instructed them to wait precisely forty minutes, but it felt like days to Barmy before Ben said soberly, "Come on, Barmy – our turn now."

Twenty-four

The tunnel was enormous, stone-flagged, stone-lined and with a high, vaulted ceiling. The whole thing was extremely badly lit. Wrought-iron wall brackets hung at regular intervals, but only some were set with torches and of these, not all had managed to remain lit in the steady draught.

Despite Facecrusher's comments about ghoul patrols, security checks and pilgrims coming for Tanaka's birthday celebrations, they had seen no one since they entered the tunnel, and plodded through the gloom with no company but their own footsteps and the infernal wind. It took only minutes of this to set Barmy's nerves on edge. Ben, on the other hand, seemed as imperturbable as ever.

"Facecrusher has a very special interest in Castle Tanaka, Barmy," Ben began. "Not many people know this, but she – " He stopped abruptly, not only speaking but moving, so that Barmy walked straight into his back.

"Wha – ?"

"Shhhhh!" Ben said.

Barmy shushed and listened, his nerves, already badly strained, now teetered at breaking point. Eventually, very quietly indeed, he asked, "What is it, Ben?"

"I think it might be a ghoul patrol, Barmy," Ben said. "Can't you hear them?"

"No." He heard nothing, nothing at all but the wind.

"I think they're up ahead, coming this way. I might be wrong, of course, Barmy, but I think we should put our hoods up and pretend to be pilgrims." He pulled his hood over his head and adjusted it so that he could see out through the eye slits. "Now, Barmy, best foot forward and remember they can only kill you once."

Not at all comforted, Barmy arranged his own hood.

Ben's hearing must have been exceptionally acute for it was almost five minutes before they encountered the ghoul patrol. A little ahead of time, Barmy heard the slap-slap of bare feet on flagstones, occasionally broken by the curious grunting chirps with which ghouls signalled one another. Then, with dreadful finality, the patrol emerged out of the gloom.

There were perhaps fifteen or twenty of the creatures, some upright, some loping almost on all fours, knuckles brushing the ground like apes. But unlike any other ghouls Barmy had yet seen, they were armed. Above the tattered loincloths they all seemed to wear was a leather harness which enabled each to carry a sword, dagger and a smallish shield. In some, the sword had been replaced by a spiked chain mace. The group halted as it caught sight of Ben and Barmy.

Without the slightest hesitation, Ben walked towards them. After a moment of confusion, Barmy followed. When they were only a few metres distant, Ben raised his right arm in a passable imitation of the old Hitler salute and said loudly, "Hail Tanaka! Hail Obedniga!"

"Hail Tanaka! Hail Obedniga!" Barmy echoed. As an afterthought, he too raised his arm. The ghouls had spread out in a triple line to block their way. The lead ghoul sprang forward, snarling, drew a sword, then crouched to slap its flat side on the ground, sending up a ringing, metallic challenge which reverberated up and down the tunnel. The creature threw its head back and emitted a single, savage scream. To Barmy's horror, Ben kept walking.

The remaining ghouls began to snarl and scream as well, their eyes glinting fiercely in the gloom. Several began to leap up and down, grunting, screeching and flailing their arms in menace and excitement.

Barmy took it all in with mounting terror. According to the Reverend Bong, with whom he had discussed ghouls on the march, these creatures had no language and a level of intelligence far below that of even the most primitive human. Given patience and a little magical control, they could sometimes be trained to use simple tools and fight with weapons, but they were utterly unpredictable and frequently reverted to their fundamental instinct, which was to savage everything in sight and eat it.

The leading ghoul stood up, stretched out both arms (sword still firmly clutched in its right hand) and stepped out to block Ben's passage forward. More and more ghouls began to draw their weapons. The air was suddenly filled with metallic noise, interspersed with snarls and grunts and screams.

"Eeeeeeeyah!" screamed the lead ghoul, making a warning gesture with four wriggling fingers placed to one side of his left eye.

"Hail Tanaka!" Ben said loudly – and brushed the creature to one side with an impatient sweep of his empty hand.

The remaining ghouls parted like the sea before a ship as Ben walked firmly forward with Barmy pressed in at his back. The ghouls closed around them in an excited mob, chattering and snarling, screaming and gesticulating. Hands reached out to pluck at their clothing, touch their hair, but to Barmy's absolute bewilderment, no fangs snapped, no weapons slashed.

For an eternal moment, all was activity and noise, then they passed through the ghastly tribe and were walking briskly down the tunnel with the ghoul patrol receding in the distance.

When the gloom had swallowed them completely, Ben threw back his hood. "Piece of cake, Barmy," he remarked. "Now comes the hard part."

Twenty-five

"I think there's a security check ahead," Ben said.

After a moment, Barmy asked, "Do we have papers, Ben?"

"Oh yes," Ben said, "Facecrusher fixed all that up. She gave every member of the party papers. She gave me yours and mine. There's no problem about that, Barmy, no problem at all. The only problem is I forgot to bring them."

Barmy stared at him. "You forgot?"

"I'm sorry, Barmy."

Barmy shook his head. "What do we do now, Ben?"

Ben grinned suddenly. "I have a plan, Barmy. You stay here and I'll sneak up ahead and suss out how the land lies. Then I'll come back."

He waited.

And waited.

Maybe he should have followed Ben after all. He was gone a long time. Too long. Far too long.

He waited.

Something tugged at his sleeve. Barmy started violently and only just stopped himself from screaming.

"It's only me, Barmy," Ben said at his elbow.

"What happened, Ben?" Barmy asked anxiously.

Ben grinned sheepishly. "Oh yes, I nearly forgot." His face set in a sober expression. "It's bad news, Barmy. The others have been captured."

"Captured? All of them?"

"I think Pendragon may still be free, but the others have all been taken away to the Baron's dungeons. It seems their papers were wrongly dated." He looked up at Barmy with an open smile. "Lucky I forgot ours, eh, Barmy?"

"How did you find all this out?"

"I lurked," said Ben. "If you lurk long enough you nearly always hear something interesting. All the guards were talking about it."

"What are we going to do now, Ben?"

"Don't worry, Barmy, I have another plan," he said. "We'll sneak into the castle another way without using the tunnel. That way we can avoid the security checks."

"Facecrusher said the tunnel was the only way in," Barmy protested.

"Facecrusher isn't a dwarf," Ben told him.

No arguing with that, but Barmy tried anyway. "What do you mean?"

"There's no way in for normal sized people – no other way, I mean: they have to come through the tunnel. But if you're a dwarf, there's a crawlspace you can use."

"You're sure?"

"Oh, yes," Ben said.

Barmy blinked. He was taller than Ben, though not so broad. "What about me? Will I be able to get through?"

"I think you might, Barmy. I don't know for sure, but we could always try. I've got some butter in my backpack."

"Butter?" Barmy echoed in bewilderment, staring at the little lunatic beside him.

"In case you get stuck, Barmy," Ben smiled.

After a moment, Barmy said, "Where is it – this crawlspace?"

"Not far," Ben promised, and started back along the tunnel in the direction they had come.

Twenty-Six

It was a nightmare, the sort that made his worst experiences in the tunnel feel like a vicar's tea party. The crawlspace was pitch black, narrow, low, damp, claustrophobic and filled with slithery things that brushed against you when you least expected it.

Ben kept up a running commentary of utterly inane encouragement that was driving Barmy close to homicide by the time he caught sight of a faint glimmer of grey light ahead which changed his mood at once.

"Look, Ben – we're nearly through!" he hissed.

"Not quite, Barmy," Ben said. "But it will be a bit easier now."

He was right on both counts. They emerged from the crawlspace into a cramped, square shaft illuminated by the barest filtering of light.

"This is the ventilation system," Ben explained. "It, goes all over the castle, so we can get to anywhere from here but you have to keep very quiet because sound carries though it."

"Where are we trying to get to?"

"I thought we should try to rescue the others first, then look for your alchemist."

"We don't know where the others are, do we?" asked Barmy.

"Not for certain, but chances are they're locked up in the dungeons. That's what happens to you when you're captured."

"But how do we know which way?" whispered Barmy.

Even in the gloom he could see the shaft they had entered branched in half a dozen places.

"Just follow me," said Ben, "I know these shafts like the back of my hand."

Barmy followed. They had gone a considerable distance before he thought to ask, "When we find them, how do we get them out, Ben?" Aspen and Rowan might – just – have fitted into the ventilation shafts: the rest never would. And even Aspen and Rowan would have had real problems in the crawlspace.

"Don't you worry, Barmy," Ben reassured him. "I have a plan. When we find them, we'll fight our way out."

Barmy closed his eyes. He seemed to be on another suicide mission. "What about Kendar?"

After a moment, Ben said, "You mustn't expect me to work out all the details, Barmy. Why don't you try to think of something?"

In the event it did not matter since Ben, who knew the ventilation system like the back of his hand, got them lost.

The shaft opened into the equivalent of a small cupboard, so that they were able to crouch side by side, their noses pressed against a finely meshed metallic grille, looking down into an opulent bedchamber furnished in barbaric splendour.

"This doesn't look like dungeons," Barmy hissed.

"No, it doesn't," Ben agreed. He was picking at the mortar round the metal grille. Carefully he removed the grille. "We'll just nip down and take a closer look, Barmy." Ben dropped down and was looking up at him with encouraging gestures.

"Come on, Barmy, it's not far to jump."

A sort of grim fatalism gripped Barmy's stomach. Why should he worry – it was all mad anyway. He swung out of the shaft and dropped down nimbly, then drew his sword.

"That's a good idea, Barmy," Ben said, "in case any-body comes." He drew his own sword in imitation. "Now let's search this place and try to find out where we are."

It was, Barmy quickly discovered, a woman's bedroom. There were three doors, each constructed from heavy oakwood and leading heaven only knew where. With infinite caution, Barmy opened one of them and found himself staring into a tiled bathroom where three marble steps led down into a sunken pool at each corner of which were things like dolphins cast in iron, their mouths open.

He closed the door again and tried the one beside it, opening it no more than a crack until he was certain nothing ghastly lurked behind it. It led into a walk-in wardrobe which confirmed his conclusion that this was a woman's bedroom. It was, Barmy saw at once, the wardrobe of a very small woman, perhaps even a dwarven lady, although the tunics, robes and gowns all seemed a little slim fitting for that. He turned towards Ben, then froze.

Ben was standing by the bed, a small black book in his hand. The colour had drained from his face so that he looked like his own corpse and he was visibly trembling.

"What's wrong, Ben? What's the matter?" Barmy asked in sudden alarm.

Ben swallowed hard and pointed at the book. "It's a diary," he said.

Barmy waited.

"Do you know whose bedroom this is, Barmy?" Ben asked, still trembling. Then, without waiting for the answer, he said, "It belongs to Obedniga, that's who!"

The news left Barmy cold. The bedroom had to belong to somebody and as long as they weren't found in it, he was happy enough. "So what, Ben – she's not here."

"She doesn't have to be!" Ben hissed. "She's Tanaka's war witch! She wouldn't leave her chamber without magical protection. Everything we touch in here will have a curse on it. We're doomed!" The book fell from nerveless fingers and he stepped forward to grip the lapels of Barmy's tunic. "Doomed, I tell you, Barmy! Doomed! Doomed!"

"Pull yourself together, Ben!" Barmy snapped, giving him a little shake. "You're just frightening yourself. You've absolutely no reason to believe anything we've touched is cur – "

"Doomed!"

" – sed." He gripped Ben's shoulders. "Do you feel any different since we came in here?"

"Doomed!"

"Ben, do you feel any different?"

After a moment Ben said reluctantly, "No."

"No pains, no aches, no disorientation, no bits falling off?"

"No."

"There you are then!" Barmy said. "If she was going to lay a curse, it would be something that would act at once." He let go of Ben's shoulders to spread his arms. "So – no curse! That makes sense, doesn't it?"

"I suppose so," Ben said uncertainly.

"Of course it does!" said Barmy quickly. "Let me put it to you another – " He stopped. The handle of the third door, the one he had not yet tried, was turning. Hide! his mind said, but his body and his tongue were paralysed.

"What's the matter, Barmy?" Ben asked, blinking. Behind Ben's back, the door began to swing silently open.

"Ah-do – ah-do – ah-dooooor – " said Barmy, swallowed by a sudden wave of terror.

The door opened fully and a slim, small figure walked in with the brisk, confident step of a war witch entering her bedroom. Ben twisted round and immediately his eyes turned upwards as if he were about to faint. "Obedniga!" he gasped. Then, in a lunatic attempt to pretend he was a pilgrim, added, "Hail Obedniga!"

But it was not Obedniga, although Barmy almost wished it had been. He closed his eyes tight for an instant, then finding the figure still there and unchanged when he opened them, stumbled over to the bed and sat down heavily.

"You took your time getting here," the figure said shortly. "And I'll thank you not to mess up the covers on my bed."

With the voice, the last faint remnant of doubt disappeared. She was richly dressed in unfamiliar robes, but she was definitely his sister Lauren.

Twenty-seven

A feeling of relief, as unexpected as it was overwhelming, flooded over him like a tidal wave. Against all reason, he felt that now, somehow, everything would be all right. He thought he might get home. He bounced from the bed like a ball and threw his arms around her. "Boy!" he said, "am I glad to see you!"

Lauren's nose wrinkled delicately. "You smell awful, Barmy. If I didn't know better, I'd swear you'd smeared yourself with rancid butter."

"Never mind that," Barmy said. "What are you doing here? How did you get here?" Then, remembering the only really worthwhile question, "Do you know how to get back?" He reckoned there was an even money chance she'd say yes to the last. Lauren had a habit of knowing how to do things other people didn't.

But in fact she said, "No, I don't know how to get back – yet. I'm working on it. I got here by following you."

"Following me?" Barmy frowned.

"I do hope you're not going to repeat everything I say the way you usually do," Lauren told him. "When I heard that stupid story about the old Logan place, I knew you were bound to investigate – "

"How?" Barmy asked furiously. His initial upsurge of affection towards Lauren had vanished, replaced by the old irritation.

"I know you," Lauren sighed. "You're perfectly predictable. In any case, you did investigate and knowing you can never take care of yourself properly – "

"Of course I can take care of myself prop – "

" – I followed you. Naturally, you never noticed I was there – "

"Of course I knew you were there!" Barmy lied. "I knew right from the – "

" – so when you started that ridiculous walk of yours down the stairs, I saw you disappear." She sniffed. "It was a moderately interesting phenomenon, which I assumed to be associated with some sort of rift in the Einsteinian space/time continuum, so I followed quickly before the rift closed and I found myself here."

"Up a tree in an oak forest," Barmy said.

Lauren frowned. "No. No, not at all. I emerged in the great hall of Castle Tanaka. Did you find yourself up an oak tree?"

Barmy nodded. "Yes."

"How interesting."

"Excuse me, Madam Obedniga," Ben put in nervously, bowing a little. "My name's Ben and this is my friend Barmy Jeffers, who though young is a lethal fighting machine capable – "

"She knows who I am, Ben!" Barmy hissed. "She's my sister. And she's not Tanaka's war witch Obedniga, so you don't have to – "

Lauren coughed. "As a matter of fact . . ."

Barmy stared at her. From out of the depths of his soul a horrid realization emerged. "You *are* Obedniga?"

"Yes. Yes, I am."

"But how?" Barmy wailed. It was unendurable. His rotten little sister had followed him – *followed him* – through the warp and before he could turn round had established herself as one of the most powerful people in the country. It was a bit much that she'd allied herself with somebody as evil and repulsive as Baron Tanaka, but Lauren always made her own rules and the achievement was impressive just the same.

121

"How? Don't you ever use your head, Barmy? This is an essentially primitive society. Decidedly low tech. Look at the weapons – swords and maces and the occasional halberd. Not a machine-gun in the entire army. The most advanced thing they have is a crossbow. Anybody with the slightest inkling of high technology can impress these people from here to kingdom come. They think the simplest machine is magic and the woman who designs it for them is a witch." She scratched the side of her nose. "Of course, appearing out of nowhere in the great hall helped. The Baron always thought his castle was impregnable."

"Why Obedniga?" Barmy asked. "Why did you want to take on a – "

"Why not? You need an impressive name when they make you a war witch. Can you imagine a crowd shouting Hail Lauren Jeffers?"

Barmy felt utterly deflated. Here he was, an adventurerer in a totally different reality, and he still couldn't get away from his sister.

"Are you really Barmy's sister?" Ben asked uncertainly.

Lauren nodded. "Unfortunately."

"Then maybe you can help us," Ben said. "Barmy is now part of a courageous, experienced and resourceful adventure party who have been accidentally captured by your Baron Tanaka and – "

"He's not my Baron Tanaka," Lauren put in coldly. "I can't stand that creature. I've purely been playing along until I could find some means of getting home."

"Do you have an alchemist here called Kendar?" Barmy asked.

" – are being held somewhere in the castle, probably the dungeons and we – "

"One at a time!" Lauren said firmly. "Are you talking about Facecrusher's people, Ben?"

"That's right, Madam Obedniga," Ben said.

"Facecrusher's with the Baron, of course. The other four are in the dungeons."

"Other five," Barmy said. "There were six in the party altogether."

"Only five were captured," Lauren said. "A cleric, a wizard, a thief, Facecrusher and the other fighter."

"Fighter?" Barmy asked. "Male or female?"

"Female – quite a young woman."

So Pendragon was on the loose. Barmy wondered where he'd got to. "Are they all right?" he asked. Specifically he wanted to ask if the other fighter was all right, but he knew Lauren would be onto the implications like a rat up a spout. Not that he was all that worried about Aspen any more. From what he'd seen, she'd proved the toughest of the bunch.

"As all right as anybody ever is in a dungeon," Lauren sniffed. "Dark, damp, cold and poorly fed, but apart from that it's the Ritz."

"Don't you get sarcastic with my friend, Barmy, otherwise I'll bash you, Madam Obedniga," Ben said.

They both stared at him in astonishment. He stared back levelly. Eventually, to Barmy's absolute amazement, Lauren muttered, "Sorry."

"That's all right," Ben said. "Can you help us rescue our friends?"

"I think so," Lauren told him. "I'm not allowed to leave the castle, but I can go anywhere I want within it. If I tell the guards I want to see the prisoners, they'll let me do it. But they won't let them go, of course." She hesitated, thoughtfully. "Unless I have written authority from Tanaka."

"If you can get us that far, we'll do the rest," Ben said confidently, obviously hatching another of his daft plans. He glanced at Barmy. "When we have the others, we can collect Facecrusher."

Barmy nodded vaguely, his mind largely on something else. "The alchemist . . ." he reminded Lauren.

"Kendar? Yes, you were asking about him. I had the Baron send him to me because I've always thought the psychological implications of alchemy are fascinating. But he turned out to be an old bore, so I let him go."

"You let him go? Where? Where's he gone?"

Lauren shrugged. "How should I know? What does it matter anyway?"

Barmy closed his eyes. "He's the one who knows about Möbius Warps!" he groaned. "He's the only chance we have of getting back to our own world!"

Twenty-eight

The dungeons were as Lauren had described them – dark, dank and distinctly unappealing. But the guards were civil enough as soon as they caught sight of Lauren's distinctive robes. Barmy could see a reputation as a war witch could carry you a long way.

"If you'll deign to come this way," one thin ruffian grovelled ingratiatingly, walking like a crab so he did not have to turn his back on them. The words were directed at Lauren, of course. Both Ben and Barmy might have been invisible for all the attention they got.

They followed him down an ill-lit corridor into an equally gloomy open chamber which smelt of bat droppings. The chamber seemed empty, although Barmy noticed a large grille set into the middle of the floor.

"Keep 'em in the pit, we do," the guard said, grinning. He snatched a lighted torch from its wall bracket, then walked across to open the grille. As it came up, he thrust the torch forward to illuminate the hole beneath and called down, "On your feet, you lot – you've got a distinguished visitor!"

Barmy leaned across to look. Blinking up at him from the bottom of a filthy, cramped pit were Aspen, Rowan, Lancelot Bong and the Amazing Presto. They looked hungry, pale, and grimy, but fit enough. Because of the position of the torch, he knew they could not see him.

"I have an order for their release," Lauren said grandly. She waved a piece of paper on which she had forged Tanaka's signature only half an hour before. Barmy held his breath.

125

"Release?" muttered the guard, twitching a little. "Nobody's ever been released from the pit before. Least-ways . . ." He rolled his eyes and grinned, ". . . not while they were still breathing! Now, if Your Ladyship would care to amuse herself by pouring a little boiling oil down, or – "

"Just get them up here!" Lauren told him in the tone of voice Barmy remembered so well.

"Shan't!" said the guard suddenly.

"What?"

"Don't have the authority, begging your pardon, M'Lady. But I'll get the sergeant." He loped off like a crab, leaving the grille open.

"Quickly!" Lauren said. "We'll get them out now before he comes back."

"What about the paper?" Barmy asked. He had been rather impressed by the forgery.

"That's only any good if they accept it right away without question. All it needs is for the sergeant to send word back to Tanaka to check and we've all had it." She was looking around hurriedly. Eventually her eyes fell on a ladder hanging from pegs on the far wall. "There it is! Barmy, give me a hand!" She ran across and started to take it down. Barmy ran to grab the other end.

Ben dropped down on one knee at the edge of the pit. "Hello, Lancie. Hello, Asprin. Hello, Rowan. I'd have thought you'd have escaped by now. Hello, Amazing. It's us. Me and Barmy and Barmy's sister the evil war witch Obedniga. We've come to rescue you. Stand clear." He pulled two daggers from his harness and dropped them into the pit. "That's in case you have to kill somebody."

"What?" Lancie's voice floated up from the pit. "That you, Ben?"

"That's right, Lancie. Just like old times when you were

126

always getting into trouble and I was always rescuing you – "

"Gangway!" Lauren said, reaching the edge of the pit with the ladder. She dropped her end over the edge. Without warning, Barmy, who had hold of the other end, almost followed it.

"Make sure it's secure," Ben told them. "Then come up in single file."

"Hold it!" Barmy hissed urgently. He had caught the sound of approaching footsteps.

Lauren caught it too. "Stay out of sight!" she called down into the pit. "We'll have to fight. Hopefully it will only be the guard and the sergeant. Can you fight?" she asked Ben.

"Yes," Ben said without elaboration. He was unslinging his ornate crossbow.

Barmy noticed she did not ask him. Grimly he drew his sword. To Ben, Lauren said, "If you're using that crossbow, may I borrow your sword?"

"All right," Ben said.

"Since when could you use a sword?" Barmy asked, still miffed by her attitude.

"Since when I had to," Lauren told him.

The grovelling guard and a burly man with sergeant's stripes stepped into the torchlight. The guard was talking quietly. The sergeant saw the drawn swords at once and shut him up with a gesture. "What's this, Obedniga?" he asked. His tone and appearance showed he was made of far sterner stuff than the guard.

"We have come for the prisoners," Lauren told him, adding in a last-ditch bluff. "On Baron Tanaka's authority. We intend to take them."

"Get them, Cecil!" snapped the sergeant without a moment's hesitation. He drew his own sword with a flourish and started forward. Cecil dropped his grovelling

127

air and followed. After three steps, both pitched forward on their faces.

"What happened?" Lauren asked.

"I shot them with my crossbow," Ben told her.

The others began to pour out of the pit. Lancelot leaped across and relieved the prostrate sergeant of his sword.

Aspen began to sprint for one of the chamber exits.

"Just a minute – " Lauren said. She hated things out of control.

Barmy ran with Aspen. "Are you all right?"

"Fine, Barmy. It's not paradise, but I've been in worse."

He found it hard to imagine, but said nothing. There was an open door in a corridor immediately outside the chamber. He could see Aspen's curious stone ball weapon lying in a corner. "I'll get it!" he called and ran ahead.

He gripped the handle, lifted it and turned back all in a single movement. Next second he was sitting on the floor. The weapon had not moved an inch. Barmy tugged again, far more cautiously this time. The chain and handle were manageable enough, but the stone ball was immobile, as if it weighed a ton. Aspen arrived, took the handle from him and swung the weapon over her shoulder.

"How did you do that?" Barmy asked, amazed, as he scrambled to his feet.

"It's tuned to me," Aspen said. "Nobody else can lift it."

Then they were running back to the others and along the corridor by which Ben, Barmy and Lauren had entered the dungeons. But they had not gone far when a tall, broad figure loomed up out of the darkness and blocked their way completely.

128

Twenty-nine

Barmy hurled himself forward without much thought, mainly because he happened to be near the front. A massive hand shot out to grip his wrist, while an equally massive arm encircled the back of his head, squishing it against the metal breastplate. His sword dropped from nerveless fingers and suddenly the pressure was released.

Barmy looked up at familiar features and realized abruptly how she had got the name of Facecrusher. His nose, released from the breastplate, felt as though it would never be the same again. "Sorry," he said.

"Good reflexes, Barmy," Facecrusher told him. She glanced around the remainder of the party. "I take it you've escaped?"

"Escaping, dear lady," the Bong said. "Escaping."

"What's the war witch doing with you?" Her voice was calm enough, but Facecrusher's eyes were wary.

Barmy, who was picking up his sword, said, "She's not a war witch – she's my sister Lauren. She's just been biding her time until she could get away from Tanaka. Lauren, this is our leader, Facecrusher."

"How do you do?" Lauren said. She might have been at a party.

"Hello, Facecrusher," Ben said. "Were you coming to rescue them, too?"

"In a manner of speaking, Ben," Facecrusher said. "I persuaded Filbert to release them."

Barmy frowned. "Filbert?"

"Baron Tanaka," Ben said. "It's his first name."

Barmy looked at Facecrusher, then at his friends in the

adventure party. There was something going on here he did not understand. Facecrusher seemed to know all about the castle and its defences. She hadn't been thrown into the pit with the rest of the party. And now she was calling Baron Tanaka by his first name. "Excuse me, Facecrusher," he said politely, "do you know the Baron?"

For a moment there was total silence, then, with the exception of Lauren, everybody started laughing. Barmy looked round in bewilderment.

"She's married to him, Barmy," Ben said finally.

Barmy felt his jaw drop to a level somewhere near his knees. "*Married* to . . . ?" No wonder she had been so easily persuaded to come after the alchemist Kendar: her party must have been the only one in the entire country with a chance of surviving in the castle.

"Her real name's Lady Tanaka," the Bong said grinning.

"I don't use the title," Facecrusher explained a little unnecessarily.

"She likes Facecrusher better," the Bong said; and everybody was doubled up again in merriment.

When they recovered, Aspen said, "We did in two guards back there, Facecrusher. Do you think the Baron will mind?"

She shook her head and shrugged bitterly. "What's a couple more corpses to him?"

"Facecrusher doesn't get on with her husband," Ben whispered to Barmy.

"Well," said the Bong, briskly, "Tally-ho and let's get out of here while the going's good, what?"

But Facecrusher was chewing her bottom lip. "We can try, Lancie, but there could be a problem . . ."

"We'll have to find old Draggie, who's wandering around loose somewhere – "

"No, I wasn't thinking of Pendragon – "

130

" – and, of course, Barmy still wants to get his grubby little hands on Kendar, but he's left now so we're going to have to track him, but – "

Facecrusher was looking at Lauren. "Actually," she said, "the problem will be taking you along."

Barmy went very still inside.

"When I asked him to let Lancie and the others go, he was piggish about it, but that's because he's piggish about everything. He fiddled round and said no and made me wait because it's his nature to upset people. I wasn't worried and eventually when he'd had his fun, he agreed." Her eyes had not left Lauren and suddenly her voice was very sober. "But he's not going to let his war witch go so easily."

"She's not a war witch!" Barmy said heatedly. "I told you she's – "

"Shut up, Barney," Lauren told him calmly. To Facecrusher, she said, "Please go on."

"He told me a lot about you, Obedniga. He's very impressed by you. He thinks you're worth your weight in platinum. How did you do it?"

"She showed him some stupid tricks from our reality," Barmy muttered. There was panic clawing at his stomach. Whatever their differences, he didn't want to be separated from Lauren again now that he'd found her here. She might be difficult and uppity, but she was still his sister. Besides – and he admitted it to himself with the utmost reluctance – he felt a little safer with her around.

To his surprise, Lauren nodded. "That's about what I did," she said.

"Well," said Facecrusher, "they worked. All too well, by the sound of it. If you're to come with us – "

"Of course she's to come with us!" Barmy realized he was almost shouting and repeated more quietly, "Of course she's to come with us."

" – he's going to make trouble. And my husband can

131

make a lot of trouble. Does he know where you are now?"

Lauren shook her head. "No, but I imagine he could find out I've gone missing any time."

"Once that happens," Facecrusher said, "there's no question of my protecting you – protecting any of you – or myself, come to that. Filbert is quite mad – "

"That's true," the Bong put in, talking to no one in particular. "The only sane thing he ever did was marry Facecrusher – and that didn't last."

" – and when anybody tries to take away anything he considers his, he can be very extreme."

"But we can't leave Lauren behind!" Barmy said, a little widly. To his relief, he saw heads nodding agreement.

"I have a plan," Ben said. He looked around and grinned like a conjurer who has just produced the rabbit. "We'll sneak out of the castle."

After a moment, Facecrusher said, "that sounds as good a plan as any."

But they had not gone more than a few hundred metres before an alarm bell began to toll, its brittle notes reverberating through the castle like a death knell.

Thirty

They ran.

In Barmy's mind, one stone-flagged corridor blended into another without distinction until he felt he was fleeing through a maze. Only instead of ghosts pursuing him, he knew he would be chased by Tanaka's men.

"This way!" Facecrusher called. She seemed to know what she was doing, for so far they had encountered no guards and the only indication of how perilous their situation had suddenly become was the continued ringing of the bell.

"Where are we going?" asked the Bong, whose long, loping stride had taken him to Facecrusher's side. "I could be wrong, dear lady, but I don't think this route will take us outside."

"It won't," Facecrusher told him. "I'm worried about the monster kennels."

"Oh dear," Ben said.

"What are the monster kennels?" Barmy asked in sudden panic. "Ben, what are the – "

"So soon?" This from the Bong. "You think he'll open them so soon?"

"It's where I left him." Nobody had to be told she meant the Baron.

"I thought he only used the monsters as a last resort!" Rowan called cheerfully. It was the first time he had spoken since the rescue and nobody answered him.

"So did I," said the Bong, echoing Rowan. "Or does it depend on his mood?"

"Depends on his mood," Facecrusher confirmed. "I have a plan," she added.

"She has a plan," Ben echoed. He grinned. It was obvious he liked plans.

They had emerged from the dungeons and crossed an open courtyard, but now they reached a broad flight of stone steps and started to run down them to a lower level.

They were underground again, but unlike the dungeons which were damp and dark, these corridors were well lit, dry and increasingly warm. A hot, baked wind blew up from somewhere beneath, so that the further they ran, the greater the impression of moving into a gigantic oven. The wind carried a curious mixture of smells, sulphurous and rank.

"Pardon me, Facecrusher," Lauren said, "but aren't we going towards the monster kennels now? This looks like one of the entrances to the caverns."

"Towards what?" Barmy panicked.

"That's right," Facecrusher called back over her shoulder to Lauren. They're quite close now."

Five men at arms appeared in a tight group up ahead, but the party cut through them like a scythe through wheat. Lancelot paused just long enough to relieve one of them of a mace, then loped to catch up with his companions.

They were, Barmy realized suddenly, no longer running through man-made corridors, but along a tunnel cut through natural rock. The heat had risen to a point where it was almost unendurable and up ahead he could see a steady, roseate glow.

"Why are we going towards the monster kennels, Facecrusher?" Ben asked. If the prospect worried him, it did not show.

"My plan, Ben," gasped Facecrusher, definitely quite winded now.

The tunnel opened without warning into the first of a series of vast natural caverns and Barmy saw at once the source of the glow and the heat. Lava streams, presumably the source of those he had seen above on the approach to the castle, criss-crossed the cavern floor. Lava pools bubbled like sullen kettles. Fumeroles belched blue-grey smoke which cast a pall throughout the entire cavern.

Facecrusher stopped and raised one hand. The others stumbled to a halt, their faces suggesting they were glad of the opportunity to catch their breaths.

After a panting moment, Facecrusher said. "We're only a few caves away from the monster kennels – " She paused to wipe away the sweat that was streaming from her brow. "Some – some of you may be wondering why – why I led you here. The fact is, none of us had the slightest chance of leaving the castle alive once the alarm sounded. Filbert has an army of guards and an army of ghouls and both go on the rampage when that bell sounds. We didn't meet many coming this way, but don't fool yourselves – the outer reaches of the castle, the exit corridors, will be swarming with them. There is no way we could have avoided detection or fought our way through."

"But you have a plan, Facecrusher," Ben said cheerfully.

"Yes, Ben, I do. It's dangerous, but it's the only chance we've got. Filbert is a very impatient man. If he doesn't hear we've been captured quickly, he'll open the traps of the monster kennels. The things inside will fly and crawl and run and slither all through the castle inside three quarters of an hour – "

Things? Barmy thought. What sort of things? Sensibly, for once, he did not ask.

135

"Once that happens," Facecrusher went on, "everything is chaos. The point is, if we couldn't escape because of the guards and the ghouls, once the traps are open there is not the slightest chance we could even survive."

"So we've come to the kennels to stop him opening the traps?" Ben said. "That's a good plan, Facecrusher."

"Thank you, Ben, but that's not quite all there is to it. The only way I can see us escaping now is by snatching Filbert as a hostage."

In the silence there was a thudding noise that only Barmy heard. It was the sound of his heart dropping directly into his boots.

Thirty-one

It was not what he expected. Somewhere in the back of his mind he had had a picture of rows of cages filled with monsters like a dog pound or a dreadful zoo. Instead, he and his companions followed Facecrusher through a series of interlinking caverns.

As Barmy entered the first cavern, he felt his stomach tighten. The creature in it wasn't particularly large, but its very appearance was enough to strike terror into his heart. He could not even imagine himself fighting it, let alone winning any sort of conflict. Fortunately he did not have to. The loathsome creature was confined by a barred gate of strong metal. It watched them hungrily as they passed, multiple eyes glinting. Barmy noticed the gate was on rollers, attached to some mechanism high up in the roof of the cave. Obviously it could be raised or lowered at will.

Facecrusher must have caught his expression, for she called out as if talking to the party in general, "Don't worry – Filbert is the only one who can release them; and he won't do that for a little while yet."

Barmy was not reassured, but he pressed on. There was nothing else he could do.

The first cave led on to another with its own prowling shape – behind steel bars – dramatically different from the first, but no less horrible. And the second cave led to a third, which housed a small pack of six creatures. And the third led to a fourth where the bars confined something the size of a small bear.

The scent of the creatures was rank, but as they passed

137

from cave to cave, Barmy found he could no longer smell it.

They moved quickly, driven by the knowledge there was not much time to lose. Barmy had lost count of the number of caves they passed through before Facecrusher led them into a passageway and halted them with a signal.

"Quietly from now on," she said softly. "There are ghoul guards at the end of this tunnel. Not many, so we should dispatch them easily, but I don't want to alert Filbert, so it has to be done without noise. Once we pass the guard post, we enter a large cavern where we will certainly find Baron Filbert Tanaka. Unfortunately we will also find the control mechanism which can open every monster cage down here. And Filbert will use it without hesitation if he feels himself under threat."

"So what's the strategy?" Lancelot Bong asked. "Bless 'em, bash 'em, hack 'em, slash 'em?"

"Something more subtle's needed," Facecrusher grinned. "First the ghoul guards – Aspen, you're the best fighter we have. I want you to go ahead and take care of them very quietly indeed. Can you manage on your own or do you want someone with you?"

"How many ghouls?" Aspen asked.

"Five," Facecrusher said.

"I'll go alone."

"How long will you need?"

"Give me ten minutes since it has to be done quietly."

"I'll give you five," Facecrusher said soberly. "We don't have ten. But I still want it done quietly."

Aspen grinned at her, unslung her curious stone weapon and made off down the corridor without another word.

They squatted in the passage, each one lost in thoughts. Finally, Facecrusher gave the signal and they moved out after Aspen. After fifty metres, Facecrusher ordered all

138

torches extinguished and they pressed forward slowly in almost total darkness. Barmy felt a hand take his own, and recognized it as that of Lauren, although whether she was seeking comfort or just making sure he did not get himself lost he could not tell.

After an age, Facecrusher issued a whispered command to halt. They froze, and as they did so, Barmy became aware of something approaching down the passage. He held his breath and tightened his grip on his sword. There was an odd staccato clicking, like two pebbles tapped together. At once Facecrusher said, "It's all right – it's Aspen." A shape loomed up and it was.

"Done," Aspen said. "Don't trip over the bodies."

"Well done," Facecrusher hissed. "This is where it gets a little hairy. We have to grab Filbert before he can release the monsters. That's not going to be easy. He may look like a great fat slob, but he has ways of hurting people you can hardly imagine. Chances are he will be near the control mechanism – "

"He is," whispered Aspen. "I risked a peek."

" – so should he get the slightest hint of anyone approaching, he will use it. If he does, we're finished. The monsters will congregate on the control cavern before spreading out through the castle. Anything they find in there won't stand a chance."

"So what's your plan, Facecrusher?" Ben asked.

"Two possibilities," Facecrusher said briskly. "Our best shot is magic. Could you bind him, Presto?"

"Not unless you can get these things off," said the Amazing Presto, holding out his hands in the gloom. For the first time since the rescue, Barmy noticed he was wearing heavy manacles.

"Not without making noise," Facecrusher told him sourly. "Pity you didn't mention them sooner."

"Sorry," Presto said, managing to sound miffed.

139

"All right," said Facecrusher, "no magic – we're going to have to do it the hard way. We go into the cavern singly with a thirty second gap between us. You'll see Filbert and the control mechanism easily enough: there are a lot of lighted torches and some lava flows. But it's a large cavern and there are plenty of shadows and rocky outcrops and places to hide. Which is exactly what I want you to do. Slip in quietly, one at a time, and hide. Then make your way as close to the Baron as you possibly can without being spotted. Then wait. I'll be the last. When I'm in position, I'll call out the order to attack. Don't hesitate – just get him! With luck, some or all of us will be close enough to grab him before he can release the monsters. Any questions?"

There was silence.

"Any comments?"

"That's a good plan, Facecrusher," Ben said.

"Thank you, Ben."

One by one, at thirty second intervals, they began to move off down the passage.

Thirty-two

Barmy froze. The cavern was vast, but he saw Tanaka immediately, picked out in the central pool of light thrown up by a criss-cross of narrow lava flows. He was huge and ugly. The monstrous statue in the temple had, if anything, been flattering. He was alone and apparently unarmed, pacing impatiently. Nearby – and certainly within easy reach – was a large lever attached to some mechanical device. It took Barmy no time at all to work out this was the control which would release the monsters.

He could see the logic of Facecrusher's plan. Although the lava flows illuminated the centre, the entire perimeter of the cavern was in deep shadow and there were parts in absolute darkness. And there were a hundred hiding places – rocky outcrops, basalt pillars, crystalline extrusions from both floor and ceiling, fissures, caves and niches galore. From the passageway through which Barmy had entered, a causeway led directly to Tanaka, its line picked out clearly by twin rows of mounted torches. Two similar causeways, similarly lit, stretched to what he took for alternative entrances and exits.

Barmy realized he was standing like an idiot in a pool of light thrown up by the causeway torches and unfroze promptly to dart sideways like an insect into the gloom. He was the third in line to go – both Ben and Aspen were ahead of him – but could see no sign of the others.

Taking great care not to make a sound, he began to move closer to Tanaka.

He would have been happier, frankly, had it been a fight to the death. But the plan, of course, was to take

141

Tanaka alive and use him as a hostage until they could quit the castle. It was not going to be easy, even with a totally coordinated effort.

He pushed the doubts and worries from his mind and tried to think positively. It was not easy with that ugly brute pacing only yards away.

Somebody was walking down the causeway!

A guard stopped beside the towering Tanaka and saluted crisply.

"Well?" Tanaka growled.

"No sign of her yet, sir. No sign of any of them."

"But they have not left the castle?" He had one of those resonant voices that reverberated throughout the cavern.

The guard shook his head. "No, sir."

"My beauties will get them," Tanaka murmured. He turned and actually caressed the lever. "Report back in fifteen minutes with the latest position," he told the guard. "Then we'll see!"

"Sir!" said the guard, saluted and marched off. Out of the corner of his eye, Barmy saw the smallest flicker of movement by the entrance and calculated that by this time Facecrusher must be in position. He gripped his sword more tightly and tried to calm the pounding of his heart. The time for action had come.

An armoured figure appeared on the causeway, running.

It was Pendragon! Barmy recognized the shape at once. Behind him scuttled a small, thin man in maroon wizard's robes, arms waving, mouth chanting an incantation. Tanaka whirled around, his eyes took in the situation and his hand reached out for the metal lever.

The broad figure of Facecrusher rose up out of the shadows like some sea monster emerging from the deep. The little man in wizard's robes stopped dead at the sight

142

of her, then backed off in fright. His heel caught a pebble and he fell, hitting his head on a rock.

"Attack!" she roared.

Barmy jumped forward, vaguely aware of other movements in the cavern. But it was too late, all too late. Long before anyone could reach him, Tanaka jerked the lever downwards, then turned and ran with astonishing speed for a man of his bulk towards an exit. The grinding sound of machinery in gear began to fill the cavern.

"Let him go!" yelled Facecrusher. "We have to stop the cages opening!" She leapt forward and began to hack with her sword at the arrangement of ropes and pulleys above the lever.

"Tally-ho!" cried a familiar voice and Lancelot Bong bounded from the shadows and promptly crashed into Pendragon.

"Idiots!" This from Aspen, running with considerable agility through what had now become an obstacle race of prone, supine and semi-conscious bodies. She reached the cage mechanism and swung her miraculous stone weapon, but it lacked the necessary cutting edge. She dropped it and swooped to pick up Pendragon's sword.

At which point Ben dropped down from a ledge above to land squarely on top of her. The breath left her body with an audible whoosh and she dropped to both knees, gasping. Ben rolled off her like a bouncing ball, but was unable to halt his momentum. One foot went directly into a lava stream which removed the boot in an explosive flash of foul-smelling smoke and burning flesh.

"Oooowwwwwwwoooooo!" Ben roared, hopping round in circles on one foot, all else forgotten.

Barmy reached the lever and swung his sword desperately, but he was just too small to reach. A figure loomed beside him and he recognized the Amazing Presto. "You do it, Presto!" he called desperately. But Presto only held out the manacles which chained his wrists to his ankles and shook his head dumbly.

Barmy jumped, sword flailing, but still could not reach the ropes that were screaming through the pulleys. Then from the outer darkness, he heard a sound like the dread, slow beat of leather wings.

And though he had never heard a sound like that before, he knew at once what it must be. The vanguard of the monsters was entering the cavern to report for duty.

Thirty-three

When Barmy was little, his mother bought him a picture book about prehistoric creatures like dinosaurs and archaeopteryxes. On the front of the book was an artist's impression of a pterodactyl, a bat-winged lizard with saw teeth, hooked talons and a nasty look in its eye. The monster which lurched into the circle of light was a bit like that, only worse. It stood about the size of an Alsatian dog with a wingspan of six feet and looked like everybody's nightmares.

Aspen launched herself towards it without a moment's hesitation.

"No!" Facecrusher screamed. "Retreat!"

For a moment Barmy thought Aspen was going to ignore her, but she halted well clear of the monster, glanced back at Facecrusher, then began to move away cautiously.

"They have magical protection," Facecrusher called. "They're almost impossible to kill with ordinary weapons."

"This isn't an ordinary weapon," Aspen called back, spinning the stone ball Barmy had not been able to lift.

"Don't risk it!" Facecrusher advised. "Our only hope is to get out by another exit – "

She stopped. Barmy followed her gaze and discovered there were no longer any other exits. Skittering down another of the causeways was something the size of a small pony, but resembling an armoured spider. The bear-thing he had noticed earlier was lumbering down the third. And even as he watched, more and more of the hellish creatures were emerging into the lighted area of the cavern, so that within seconds they were surrounded by a silent circle of pure horror.

"Forget it!" Facecrusher said tiredly "We might as well go down fighting!"

Released from her leader's orders, Aspen jumped forward and swung her weapon so that it struck the winged creature's head with a sickening thud. The thing shook itself and, apparently unhurt, lurched towards her.

"Tally-ho!" roared the Bong and loped towards something which had all the charm of a putrid jellyfish. "Bless 'em, bash 'em, hack 'em, slash 'em!"

The pain seemed to have died down in Ben's foot, for while he was standing at a slight angle on account of the missing boot, he was nonetheless calmly feeding a bolt into his crossbow. Pendragon, who may have been feeling sheepish about his flamboyant attack on Tanaka, ran to meet the bear-thing, swinging his two-handed sword.

Facecrusher lunged towards one of the largest of the monsters, a creature oozing slime from every pore. Even Rowan, who tended to stay clear of heavy action, produced two daggers and moved forward grimly, one in each hand.

As Barmy himself moved forward, clutching his sword and his terror with equal ferocity, a figure emerged from the shadows beside him and he saw it was Lauren, carrying the sword she had borrowed from Ben. For the first time he saw her as someone vulnerable and young. Depite the sword (or possibly because of it) she no longer looked like somebody who could eat Lugs Brannigan alive.

"Barney . . . ?"

"Yes, Lauren?"

"This doesn't look too good for any of us, does it?"

There was no arguing with that. "Not very, Lauren."

146

"Do you think we're going to die?"

He looked around at the ring of approaching monsters. More and more were shuffling into the cavern with every passing moment.

They neither growled, nor roared, nor snarled or made any of the sounds that normal beasts might make; and they were all the more sinister, all the more frightening, for their silence. Lancelot Bong bashed with his mace like one demented, but the creature on the receiving end kept coming forward. Ben loosed a bolt from his crossbow and though it struck with accuracy, it seemed to do no damage. The ring was closing slowly and it looked as though there was nothing any one of them could do to stop it.

Barmy shrugged. "I don't think it's looking too good," he repeated.

"I think we're all going to die," Lauren said more calmly than Barmy could have managed. "It doesn't take a genius to analyse this situation." She too glanced towards the monsters. They approached with an almost stately pace, herding the fighters before them.

We're doing to die! We're going to die! Barmy shouted in his head.

"There are a few things I've always wanted to say and somehow never got the chance."

Barmy stared at her, wondering what she was raving about. The strain might have caused her to crack up completely. The tone of voice, the stance, the attitude were nothing like the Lauren he knew. "What sort of things?" he asked suspiciously.

She glanced down at her feet, then back up at his face. "Well, only one of them's important really. I just wanted to tell you you're my big brother and I love you very much." To his profound astonishment she leaned forward and actually kissed him.

Then suddenly she was no longer with him. His head went into a vicious tailspin as he watched her run nimbly to join with Aspen in a vain attempt to hold off at least one of the monsters. She had never kissed him before, not in her whole life. She had never told him she loved him, come to that. She had stood up for him, fought for him and bullied him, but never told him . . . although maybe it all amounted to much the same thing.

He reached up to touch his cheek where she had kissed him. Of all the weirdness that had happened since he Quasimodo Walked down the Logans' stairs and into an alternative reality, that had to be the weirdest thing of all. His little sister had kissed him.

Lancelot Bong was down! A creature like a leprous ape was squatting on his chest, ripping off the breastplate in long strips as if it were so much cardboard. Ben raced forward, dropping his crossbow in favour of his sword. A barbed tail lashed out, catching Facecrusher so that she doubled up, stumbled and fell like a tree. At once three of the smaller monsters were upon her. Aspen gave vent to a strangled scream and he saw something had a suckered tentacle around her throat. Lauren hacked vainly to free her. There was no sign of Rowan, no sign of the helpless Presto, no sign of Pendragon – all three had been overtaken by the seething mass.

Barmy closed his eyes and forced himself to grip the last small fragment of calm remaining in his soul. He knew what he had to do and it frightened him even more than the encroaching monsters. He just hoped he had not left it all too late.

There was a clatter of steel on stone as Barmy dropped his sword. His eyes flickered open and his arms went up. He felt his mind lock in those dreadful psychic disciplines the Amazing Presto had worked so hard to drill into him.

From somewhere high up near the cavern roof, he thought he caught the first faint flicker of purple lights.

"Metatron habet spengler domo!" intoned Barmy in a voice that might have heralded approaching doom. "Squadrak shepla hara-hara grango!" he howled in the opening rubric of Summon Slith.

Thirty-four

Barmy's slith ripped through the fabric of reality like an express train, far larger and infinitely more terrible than the thing which had materialized so slowly above Presto's head in the market square. More to the point, it was still growing, a writhing mass of tentacles and fangs that went beyond fear into the utmost realms of inexpressible horror. Barmy wondered if he had a talent.

"Cut it off!" Almost dreamily, Barmy recognized the voice as that of the Amazing Presto. "Cut it off!"

The slith was now gigantic . . . and still growing.

"Barmy!" screamed the Amazing Presto. "*Cut it off*!"

He remembered suddenly and shut down the mantra in his mind. The slith stopped growing.

"Aaargh!" The strangled sound was drawn from Aspen, still struggling with the monster that had a suckered tentacle round her throat.

The slith rocketed towards her with such abrupt violence that there was actually a slapping sound as air rushed in to fill the space it had just vacated.

"Control it!" howled the Amazing Presto in what sounded like total panic. But the slith roared past Aspen and the nearby Lauren to hit the monster like a sumo wrestler. Almost instantly, it seemed the creature that held Aspen was being torn literally to pieces.

"Control it!" Presto yelled again, but Barmy was now well beyond such practical advice, fighting to retain even a semblance of linkage with the thing he had created.

The slith moved on, beginning a rotation as the other slith had done in the market square. For the first time, the encroaching monsters began to make a noise, a chorus of whines and grunts that merged into a rising descant of unease.

Yirp! A slith tentacle lashed out and ripped another monster to shreds. And suddenly the slith seemed to be everywhere, rending, snapping, tearing, ripping.

"Control it, Barmy!" called another voice. "Control it! Bless 'em, bash 'em, hack 'em, slash 'em!"

"Out!" Facecrusher roared. "Out!" It was an order to the party.

Tanaka's monsters were a milling panic, an embryo stampede. Yells and screams now totally drowned out the humming of the spinning slith.

Out of the corner of his eye, Barmy could see the party grouping to make good their escape, but dared not join them: he was having quite enough trouble retaining what small control he still had of the howling chaos in the cavern. He saw Pendragon scoop up his small robed companion and run with him. He noticed Aspen running arm in arm with Lauren.

There was a new sound: the earthquake crunch of shattered rock. The slith had started to tear up stalagmites by their roots and fling them with such force that they exploded and fragmented like bombs. Shards of limestone showered around Barmy, miraculously causing him no injury.

Barmy began to back away, still keeping his attention firmly focused on the slith. He was losing even the small control he had had over it; and he knew it. Sliths were a law unto themselves. You could call them up. If you were lucky you could dismiss them. But in between was murder.

The remaining monsters turned in screaming rout, racing for every hiding place and exit, trampling one another in their anxiety to distance themselves from the whirling mass of mayhem in the cavern.

"Come on, Barmy!" Aspen called. "We must get out!"

"Barney, come at once!" This was Lauren, using her obey me voice.

The activity of the slith was becoming more frenzied by the minute. It began to gouge huge craters in the granite plateau, then hurled itself with unbelievable ferocity against a rockface wall.

"It's trying to bring down the roof!" yelled Presto. "Run for your lives!"

It was enough for Barmy. What small control he had over his creation was well and truly gone. And since the party still seemed hesitant to leave without him, he took Presto's sound advice, turned and ran like mad. Behind him, now released from all constraints, the slith began to expand.

"This way!" Facecrusher yelled.

Barmy found himself running beside Ben, who ate distance with remarkable ease despite his little legs.

"That was great fun, Barmy," Ben said. "That was a very good class of slith you summoned."

Barmy was too breathless to reply.

They pounded through a corridor, aware of a heady vibration in both floor and walls and sounds behind them like the rumbling of a major earthquake.

"It's destroying the castle!" someone screamed.

Suddenly, breathlessly, they were in daylight. The noise behind was deafening. Barmy ran and ran and ran and only when exhaustion claimed him did he stop and take time to look back.

Tanaka's castle was a smoking ruin, the rock on which it perched collapsed into a rubble pile. Ghouls and humans streamed away from the debris like rats deserting a sinking ship. From the centre of it all, a huge tentacle waved feebly, the last dying twitch of a monstrous slith which had finally buried itself beneath the whole colossal structure.

"We really showed him that time, Barmy," Ben said thoughtfully.

Thirty-five

"You're . . . Kendar?" Barmy said.

"Yes."

"The alchemist Kendar?"

The little man in maroon wizard's robes nodded, then winced. He had a bump the size of a pigeon's egg growing out of the back of his skull.

"The expert on Möbius Warps?" Barmy asked cautiously. He could hardly believe it. Pendragon, the one member of the party he disliked (admittedly only because of jealousy), had found the alchemist Kendar for him.

They had set up temporary camp beyond the lava flows that surrounded Tanaka's castle – what little there was left of it. Pendragon was now something of a hero since his discovery of Kendar.

"Pendragon mentioned your problem," Kendar said briskly, while holding his head still. "I think I may be able to help you."

"You can?" asked Barmy, savagely fighting back the hope that was clawing its way up from somewhere deep inside his stomach.

"Quite easily, in fact," said Kendar, "since I have a portable warp with me."

"A portable warp?" This time it was Lauren who asked the question, frowning.

"The original warps were a natural phenomenon, young lady," Kendar said in that severe tone schoolteachers use to indicate they are discussing calculus with idiots. "But it is possible to duplicate them artificially if you have enough paper." He sniffed. "And know what you're doing."

154

"Which you do?" asked Lauren, who knew how to irritate people in such a way they could not protest.

"Yes," said Kendar irritably. "Yes, of course." He began to scrabble in a smallish leather bag and eventually drew out a strip of paper nearly three metres long. He looked around. "Is there a tree – ?"

Ben pointed silently to a stunted tree devoid of foliage some distance from the camp.

"Ah, yes," Kendar said. "That will do admirably. Thank you, little man." Ben reached for his crossbow, but Aspen caught his wrist.

Kendar trailed his paper strip to the tree where he teased it out to show it was, in fact, a paper circle, joined with the familiar Möbius twist. He found a branch parallel to the ground and hung the circle from it so that it formed a paper doorway. "There," he said.

The party followed him across, led by Barmy and Lauren. "That's it?" Barmy asked. He didn't think that was it. He could see right through the paper and everything looked exactly as it should be: no sign of his own reality, not even a shimmering in the air.

"That's it," Kendar confirmed. "Walk through the circle and you'll be back in your own world." He hesitated marginally. "If my calculations are correct . . ."

"Where in our own world?" Lauren asked suspiciously.

"That depends when you walk through," said Kendar. "Go now and you should end up reasonably near the warp you used to get here." He shrugged. "There's always a chance you might not even end up on your own planet."

"Now?" asked Barmy. Quite suddenly he did not want to go.

"Inside the next five minutes," Kendar said.

In a way, the timing was a good thing. It forced him to act. If he'd thought too much, he might have wondered why he was returning of his own free will to a world of school and people like Lugs Brannigan, when he might have stayed put with some of the finest friends he had ever known.

As it was, he made his rounds, shaking hands, while Lauren, who had said a communal goodbye, waited impatiently near the artificial warp.

"Thank you for finding Kendar, Draggie."

"Think nothing of it, young fellow," Pendragon said expansively and irritatingly. "We paladin types make a habit of helping the less fortunate."

Barmy used his left foot to keep his right boot from kicking Draggie on the shins.

"Nice meeting you, Rowan. Didn't see much of you on this adventure."

"Maybe next time," Rowan said. They shook hands then Rowan handed Barmy back his wristwatch.

Facecrusher embraced him, forcing him gently against her breastplate. "Ben was right, Barmy – you *are* a lethal fighting machine. In your own way."

"Thank you, Facecrusher. Thank you for everything."

There was a rattle as the Amazing Presto finally broke through one manacle.

"Thank you for teaching me magic, Presto," Barmy said.

"You need more practice," Presto told him sourly, glancing towards the debris of the castle.

Lancelot Bong circled Barmy's shoulder with his arm. "Don't forget the motto, what?"

"Bless 'em, bash 'em, hack 'em, slash 'em!" Barmy told him, grinning.

He went to Ben, who was seated on a rock. Much as he loved the remainder of the party, Ben was special – extra special. Barmy swallowed past a large lump forming in his throat. "Ben," he said, "I may never see you again and there's something I've wanted to say to you."

"What's that, Barmy?"

He was not even sure he should bring it up, but the tragic story of Ben's royal wife had moved him too much to leave his thoughts unspoken. "I just want you to know, Ben, how very, very sorry I am about what – " He swallowed again. " – what happened to Sheena."

Ben looked at him blankly. "Who?" he asked.

Barmy walked to Aspen and took both her hands in his. "I'll miss you, Aspen," he said truthfully.

"I'll miss you, too, Barmy," Aspen told him, looking him directly in the eyes. He hoped she would kiss him again, but she did not.

"Hurry up, Barney!" Lauren called impatiently. The tone of her voice suggested all her talk about loving her big brother had been a momentary abberation.

"Thank you!" Barmy called to the group as a whole. "Thank you all!" He was going home and he was glad. But he was sorry, too. Something deep within his heart kept wondering if there was any way he might come back. He turned and ran towards the artificial warp, grabbing Lauren's hand as he went past. "Quasimodo!" he yelled in her left ear to remind her. Together they fell into the twisted, shambling gait of Barmy's famous Quasimodo Walk.

GRAIL QUEST

Solo Fantasy Gamebooks

J. H. Brennan

King Arthur's magic realm of Avalon is besieged on every side by evil powers and foul monsters. You alone can free the kingdom from its terror, venturing forth on Quests too deadly for even the bold Knights of the Round Table. Quests that will lead you to glory — or death.

So sharpen your wits and your trusty sword Excalibur Junior, and use the intricate combat system to scheme and fight your way through the adventures in this thrilling gamebook series. A special score card and detachable easy-reference rules bookmark are included with each book.

The Castle of Darkness	**The Den of Dragons**
The Gateway of Doom	**Voyage of Terror**
Kingdom of Horror	**Realm of Chaos**
Tomb of Nightmares	**Legion of the Dead**

Armada

Horror Classic Gamebooks
by J. H. Brennan

Now you can bring your favourite horror characters to life in these spinechilling gamebooks.

Dracula's Castle

Deadly traps and evil cunning await Jonathan Harker on his arrival at the forbidding Castle Dracula. The choice is yours whether to play the fearless vampire-hunter or his arch-enemy, the vampire count himself. Will you have the stamina to survive?

The Curse of Frankenstein

Enter the ghoulish world of Frankenstein and his monstrous creation. But be warned, you will need skill, luck and nerves of steel to endure this bloodcurdling adventure.

Armada

Armadas

Here are some of the most recent titles
in our exciting fiction series:

The Chalet School and Rosalie *Elinor M. Brent-Dyer* £1.75
The Secret of the Forgotten City *Carolyn Keene* £1.95
The Masked Monkey *Franklin W. Dixon* £1.95
The Mystery of the Creep-Show Crooks *M. V. Carey* £1.95
Horse of Fire *Patricia Leitch* £1.75
Cry of a Seagull *Monica Dickens* £1.75
The Secret of Moon Castle *Enid Blyton* £1.95
Legion of the Dead *J. H. Brennan* £1.95

Armada paperbacks are available in
bookshops and newsagents, but can
also be ordered by post.

How to Order

Please send the purchase price plus 22p per book (maximum postal charge £3.00) to Armada Paperbacks, Cash Sales Dept., GPO Box 29, Douglas, Isle of Man. Please use cheque, postal or money order – do not send currency.

NAME (Block letters) ....

ADDRESS ....

....

....

While every effort is made to keep prices low, it is sometimes necessary to increase them at short notice. Collins Children's Books reserve the right to show new retail prices on covers which may differ from those previously advertised in the text or elsewhere.